I0817965

FORGET ME

(A Katie Winter FBI Suspense Thriller—Book 6)

Molly Black

Molly Black

Bestselling author Molly Black is author of the MAYA GRAY FBI suspense thriller series, comprising nine books (and counting); of the RYLIE WOLF FBI suspense thriller series, comprising six books (and counting); of the TAYLOR SAGE FBI suspense thriller series, comprising six books (and counting); and of the KATIE WINTER FBI suspense thriller series, comprising nine books (and counting).

An avid reader and lifelong fan of the mystery and thriller genres, Molly loves to hear from you, so please feel free to visit www.mollyblackauthor.com to learn more and stay in touch.

ISBN: 978-1-0943-9503-6

BOOKS BY MOLLY BLACK

MAYA GRAY MYSTERY SERIES
GIRL ONE: MURDER (Book #1)
GIRL TWO: TAKEN (Book #2)
GIRL THREE: TRAPPED (Book #3)
GIRL FOUR: LURED (Book #4)
GIRL FIVE: BOUND (Book #5)
GIRL SIX: FORSAKEN (Book #6)
GIRL SEVEN: CRAVED (Book #7)
GIRL EIGHT: HUNTED (Book #8)
GIRL NINE: GONE (Book #9)

RYLIE WOLF FBI SUSPENSE THRILLER
FOUND YOU (Book #1)
CAUGHT YOU (Book #2)
SEE YOU (Book #3)
WANT YOU (Book #4)
TAKE YOU (Book #5)
DARE YOU (Book #6)

TAYLOR SAGE FBI SUSPENSE THRILLER
DON'T LOOK (Book #1)
DON'T BREATHE (Book #2)
DON'T RUN (Book #3)
DON'T FLINCH (Book #4)
DON'T REMEMBER (Book #5)
DON'T TELL (Book #6)

KATIE WINTER FBI SUSPENSE THRILLER
SAVE ME (Book #1)
REACH ME (Book #2)
HIDE ME (Book #3)
BELIEVE ME (Book #4)
HELP ME (Book #5)
FORGET ME (Book #6)
HOLD ME (Book #7)
PROTECT ME (Book #8)
REMEMBER ME (Book #9)

PROLOGUE

The tap on Emily's window startled her. The loud, hard single knock on the darkened glass snapped her attention all the way from her phone messaging.

What was it? Had a bird flown into the window? Or was someone out there?

Feeling creeped out, as if going to look was a bad decision, but not wanting to ignore this sound, she got up from her bed and tiptoed across the room. Cautiously, she opened the curtain.

What was it? Who was out here at this hour?

She gasped as she saw a white hand slam against the glass. Then she let the breath out as she recognized the blurred, pale face beyond.

A familiar, impatient-sounding voice greeted her. "Hey, Em, c'mon, open up!"

She stared through the glass at Sandi, her friend.

Well, her sort-of friend. Tall, dark-haired, and reckless, the opposite of short, blond Emily, sixteen-year-old Sandi was one of those people she was friends with because to resist her felt kind of dangerous. Sandi lived with her mother in a tumbledown cottage on the coastline of Nova Scotia, a twenty-minute drive from the capital city of Halifax and a ten-minute walk from Emily's house.

Emily opened the window and looked out at her.

"Sandi. What is it? Is everything okay?" she asked.

"Couldn't be better right now. I got beers." Grinning, Sandi tapped her rucksack.

"You got beers? What, did you get into your mother's stash?"

Sandi didn't look sober, or at any rate, she seemed wilder than usual.

"Yes. She's out for the night," Sandi said. "So, come on, let's take a sail."

"How? Where?"

Sandi smiled slyly. "We can take your dad's rowboat and go over to that little island across the water. We can drink there. Nobody will see. It'll be fun. It's the weekend. You don't even have to get up for school tomorrow."

Emily hesitated, then said, "I don't know, I don't think it's a good idea. I'm not really supposed to go down to the beach after dark. And my dad will be totally mad if we take his rowboat."

"C'mon. I promise, I won't get you in trouble. We'll be back in a couple of hours."

With a shiver, Emily knew there was no choice here. She had—sort of—promised to do this a few days ago. She'd said she would join Sandi on a nighttime outing, anyway. But it had felt a lot different in the school cafeteria than it did now, at eight p.m. on this blustery and chilly night. And she hadn't known it would include taking her dad's rowboat.

But then, inside Emily, a sense of adventure unfurled. Why not, she thought. They could go out for an hour, drink a beer, and be back before anyone knew.

She slipped on her shoes and grabbed her jacket, zipping the phone into the pocket. Then she threw a leg over the side of the windowsill, straddled it, and climbed out, dropping to the ground.

The wind snatched at her hair. Ahead, in the gloom, she could see the bright shape of the small boat, rocking at the pier.

As they walked down to the water's edge, Sandi handed her a beer.

"Down it! Come on!" she encouraged.

Feeling as reckless as Sandi, Emily did as she was told. She snapped the can open and tipped it back.

The beer tasted cold and bitter. But Sandi's admiring laugh warmed her. They climbed into the rocking boat.

"Grab an oar. Look at the moon, how pretty it is. We can't get lost tonight," Sandi said. "You can actually see the moonlight on the beach, it looks as bright as snow. We're gonna sit there and drink these other beers together."

Emily grabbed an oar and began rowing with all her might. Sandi was right. The island wasn't far. This would be an adventure.

Only, as they headed across the narrow, turbulent strip of water, Emily found herself getting jumpy all over again. What if they'd been spotted? Wouldn't a cop or the Coast Guard or something be coming after them? Chasing them in a boat of their own? Underage drinking was a crime.

"What if someone's following us?" she said. "What if someone saw us leave?" She couldn't adequately explain the looming sense of unease she felt.

"We're okay. Nobody saw us."

She handed Emily another beer, then steered the boat with her oar as Emily tipped the can back. She drank it all down. The beer was bitter, but she was starting to really like the taste.

The moon hung above them, big and white. She could see every detail of the beach now.

And then her heart stopped as she saw someone there. Standing on the sand. A tall, dark, threatening figure.

She almost cried out in fear before her eyes adjusted to this gloomy terrain, and she realized it was just a rock.

Just a big, crooked rock, standing like a sentinel on the beach.

"You're rowing great!" Sandi cried. "We're almost there."

Her head was spinning from the beer. She felt at once reckless and terrified. The sea was rough in this stretch. The boat was plunging now, as they fought through the waves.

It was too rough. Her dad's boat might capsize or get damaged. She was sure there were rocks on the coast of this island. Abruptly, she decided enough was enough. This was a crazy idea and she wasn't going to carry on with it.

She took a deep breath, readying herself to say that they'd had enough fun, and that they must turn around and go back. But then Sandi gave a cry of alarm.

"My oar!"

With a gasp as icy water sprayed over her, Emily realized her friend had dropped her oar.

"Can you find it?" Emily cried, feeling panicked, digging her own oar in, desperately trying to slow their progress as the sea tumbled the boat to shore.

"No. It's gone!" Sandi was laughing manically. "I can't believe I did that. So clumsy of me. But we're here now, girl, we're here."

But how are we going to get back? Emily wondered. She had her phone with her, but calling the folks would mean unleashing the worst kind of trouble.

Otherwise, they were stranded. They couldn't row all the way back with just one oar.

"Come on!"

Sandi climbed out into knee-deep water, catching her breath. "Jeez, it's cold. Let's drag the boat up so it doesn't wash away, too. We can sit here a while, drink a bit. Then we can decide what to do."

This wasn't fun anymore, Emily thought, climbing out and tugging at the boat, stumbling over rocks while frigid water scoured her ankles.

This was scary and wrong. They were stuck here on a chilly night, with one oar and no means of getting home again.

"Let's find a rock and sit down and get so drunk we don't care anymore," Sandi advised.

Perhaps that was the only solution, Emily agreed, with a chill. She stared at Sandi, so lean, so tall, so sure of herself, but looking at the bigger picture, Emily realized her confidence was nothing more than bravado.

She wasn't just the wild child everyone wanted to be friends with and say yes to. She was misguided and reckless and Emily would have been a much stronger person if she'd given her a firm no.

Now, they were stranded on a cold island that felt creepy and strangely menacing.

Had it really been a rock she'd seen? she wondered again, trying to replay that moment in her mind. It had looked exactly like someone was standing there, waiting.

"I'm going to call my folks," she said. "They need to bring the motorboat to fetch us. This was a bad idea. We're going to be in such big trouble."

"Are you crazy?" Sandi glared at her without a hint of friendliness in her gaze. "If you do that, I'll never speak to you again."

"That's fine," Emily retaliated.

"Ah, come on." In a flash, Sandi had changed tack, and was sounding persuasive, her voice a coo. "Drink another beer first. Might as well hide the evidence." She opened another can.

Emily felt drunker than she had realized she was. And she urgently needed to pee.

"I'll be back in a minute. Have your beer. And then I'm calling the folks."

She stumbled away, heading away from the beach and into the forested area of this small island, her bladder painful, her eyes straining to see in the dark.

Behind her, she heard the crack of a branch and spun around, staring into the gloom.

"Who's there?"

There was no answer. But she could have sworn she saw a figure moving in the darkness.

"Sandi, is that you?"

She didn't think it was Sandi. She looked back toward the beach, but she couldn't see her friend. Just the dark waters of the sea, the moon's reflection shimmering on the rippling waves.

Then she turned, feeling her way in the dark.

And fell.

Her legs were scythed from under her by the unexpected object in her path. She landed hard on her hands, the twigs ripping at her palms, and cried out in shock and pain.

What had tripped her up?

With shaking hands she activated the light on her phone.

It illuminated the stuff of nightmares. The beam danced over a bluish-white face. Long, tangled hair. Staring, sightless eyes.

Staring down at the corpse she'd fallen over, Emily began to scream, and scream, and scream.

CHAPTER ONE

Walking up the stairs to the apartment rented by her investigation partner Leblanc, Katie Winter felt anxious and unsettled. She hoped she wasn't imposing by this unannounced visit. But she was seriously worried about him.

He'd been off work Thursday and Friday this week. He hadn't arrived at the offices used by the task force in the cross-border city of Sault Ste. Marie where they both now lived. And earlier in the week, he'd been quiet, subdued, irritable.

She'd tried to call him twice yesterday—Friday evening—and he hadn't picked up. His phone had been off.

Something was going on with him, and Katie wanted to know what. She was his colleague and case partner, and he was part of her life. If something was wrong, she wanted to help.

She paused outside his door, hoping once again she was doing the right thing by arriving on his doorstep. Then she rang the buzzer.

No answer.

She waited a minute, then tried again. Was it too early still, on this Saturday morning?

Maybe he was asleep. Or out.

Maybe he was with a woman. Katie's stomach twisted uneasily as she considered that possibility. It made her feel deeply uncomfortable to consider it, because over the past months, they had grown close. She realized she didn't want him to get involved with anyone else. That it would change the way she now thought their relationship might develop.

Her heart was hammering as she rang again.

She was just about to go away and give up on the idea when she heard footsteps in the hall. Then the lock turning. The door swung open. She stared at Leblanc in disbelief.

He was a mess. He looked disheveled and exhausted, dark rings under his eyes. His dark hair was spiked in every direction. His olive skin looked dull.

"Leblanc!" she said. "Are you okay?"

He looked everywhere but into her eyes. At the floor. Beyond her. At the purse she was carrying.

"I got back in the early hours from a trip to Paris," he said.

"Paris?" She frowned. Hadn't Leblanc been to Paris recently? She knew he'd worked there for many years, and he had mentioned something a few weeks ago about a trip to see the family of his previous investigation partner. Katie knew she had also been his lover and had been killed during a prison riot while interrogating a convict.

Now he had just been there again? No wonder his phone had been off if he'd been on a plane.

"What happened? Is there an emergency? Is anything wrong?"

She thought for a minute he wasn't going to answer. His lips got that stubborn set that she knew only too well. And then he capitulated.

"I went for a job interview."

Katie couldn't believe what she was hearing.

A job interview? Shock resonated through her.

"But—but why?" she stammered out. "What job is this?"

"It's the head of the investigation department in central Paris."

The statement blindsided her. This felt surreal. She hadn't known a thing about it. He hadn't mentioned it to her. Not one word.

"You applied for that position?"

He shrugged. "Friends told me about it. They said I would be the top candidate if I applied."

"The top candidate? That's—that's wonderful. Congratulations." Even as she uttered the reflexive words, Katie was feeling as if her world had been yanked out from under her.

"But Leblanc, tell me why," she tried. "I never knew you wanted to go back to Paris. You've only been with the task force a few months. Are you not happy here, or was this a career move you couldn't refuse, or—or what?"

Leblanc had been with the task force since its formation. He was her investigation partner. As for the Paris job, this was so far out of left field, she couldn't even think straight.

He stood there, looking as if he'd rather eat glass than deal with this conversation. And Katie noted he didn't look happy. She didn't, in fact, think this was an opportunity he was eagerly embracing.

Was there more to be uncovered?

"When was this? The interview, I mean," she probed.

"Yesterday morning." He looked away. She could see his jaw muscles clenching. "I have already been offered the job. I have the weekend to think about it and accept. Or else, on Tuesday morning, they will offer it to the next preferred candidate."

"Why didn't you tell me?" Katie quizzed him, still confused by how miserable he seemed.

"Because," he said, his voice terse and curt, "I didn't want you to know."

"Why would you want to keep it from me?" she asked, feeling a bubble of hurt.

He looked back at her. "Because," he said, a muscle jumping in his jaw, "I didn't want you to talk me out of it."

Katie looked at him more closely. Now that her shock was over, she decided that there was definitely something else going on. There was more to this. He was conflicted. That comment had just proven it. The physical tells were confirming it.

She could be as stubborn as him. And he was about to find that out.

"What's happening? Why are you doing this?"

He still had not looked directly into her eyes.

"Leblanc, is this just about the job? Is there another reason? If so, I would like to know. And I think after what we have been through, and the fact you have not told me a thing about this, I deserve to know."

There was a resounding silence.

She glanced beyond him, at his tidy apartment, noting the travel bag at the far side of the hall.

Then his shoulders slumped. "You're right," he muttered. "There's more."

He walked into the apartment. She followed him in and he motioned her to the black leather sofa.

She sat down. He didn't join her. Instead, he paced.

"You know about my investigation partner in Paris, Celeste."

Katie nodded.

"She was killed by an inmate called Hugo Gagnon," he continued. "Recently, I learned from a friend that Gagnon might be moved. If he is moved to a different prison, he will die. The prison he might transfer to is less well run. Gang members there want him dead."

Katie stared incredulously.

"What has this got to do with a job offer?" she asked.

Leblanc sighed. "I was told that the decision will fall to the new head of investigation in central Paris. So if I get the job, I will have the say. I will be able to send him there. He will get what he deserves."

He stared at Katie and in his eyes she saw a world of pain.

She empathized with the pain. But the rest of it? She felt furious. Unable to sit, she leaped to her feet.

"So this is what you say? You are basing your entire future on a revenge move so that you can manipulate a criminal who is already spending life in jail without hope of parole, into a situation where he might be murdered?"

Leblanc looked at the floor as Katie raged.

"I don't believe this! I don't believe you would sacrifice your entire future to do something like that. What were you thinking? Those are not good reasons to accept such a job, and make such a move!"

"I know," he tried, but now Katie was furious and unstoppable.

"You don't even know for sure this will happen. You've been told. Trust me, bureaucracy is alive and well in the Parisian police department. They might hand the decision to another person or postpone it a few years or rethink that nobody gets moved. And in the meantime you are upending your life! You're ending our partnership! And for what? For what?"

She spread her arms, seeing his face twist.

"There is not one positive thing in what you have said! You are mired in negativity and revenge. You are—you're freaking delusional! What even is this?"

She was close to tears.

"How could you do this? How could you even consider this? Such a cowardly move. Political maneuvering in the hope you can put a man in a situation where a fight will break out and someone will be killed. Maybe Gagnon. Maybe another convict. But you've gone behind the backs of everyone who works with you here."

There was a long silence. Leblanc looked at her, anguish in his eyes, as if her gaze was burning him.

"I'm sorry," he said, softly.

"This is not you," she whispered.

Suddenly, Katie had had enough. She marched to the door, yanked it open, and without another word, slammed it shut behind her.

She didn't look back.

Tears filled her eyes as she walked down the stairs. She blinked, but they spilled down her face.

She'd lost her temper with him. She might have said unforgivable things, but in the moment of rage she'd meant every word. Now she had no idea where they stood, or if they were even a team anymore.

And deep down, even though Katie didn't want to admit it, she understood why he desired payback. Losing a loved one was traumatic. Celeste's violent death at the hands of a killer would have deeply scarred Leblanc. But even so, taking revenge to that destructive level was wrong.

She headed out into the streets of Sault Ste. Marie, breathing in the damp, late-winter air, rain stinging her face.

This might mean an entirely new chapter of her life. She didn't want it. She wanted to go back to how things had been, but with a twist of her stomach, Katie knew that might not be possible. She might be teamed up with a new case partner. Leblanc might quit the task force on Monday.

She'd had her say and now she would have to wait for Leblanc's reaction to her words, and see whether her message had hit home hard enough to make him rethink, or whether he would sever their ties completely.

With a grace period of two days at most, she found herself dreading the outcome of his decision.

CHAPTER TWO

The next morning was gray and rainy, a somber Sunday that reflected Katie's mood.

She'd heard nothing from Leblanc, and tried to force herself to accept that every hour that passed made it more likely he'd accepted the Paris job offer.

Not wanting to agonize over that for another full day, Katie decided to spend the next few hours doing what she had vowed to pursue at all costs.

Whenever her workload allowed for a break, Katie had been spending her time looking back over her twin sister's case to see what new information she could find.

Recently, she'd received a startling eyewitness account from convicted serial killer Charles Everton, who'd been in the area when sixteen-year-old Josie disappeared after the kayaking accident.

The police had picked him up during the search for Josie, near the riverbank where she'd gone missing. Katie had always felt sure he had somehow been involved in her disappearance. Recently, when she visited him in prison for the second time, he'd admitted that he'd seen her. Everton had said Josie had been lying unconscious by the riverbank, and a tall man with dark hair and a beard had picked her up.

Katie knew she had no proof if the man was a real person or if Everton had just made him up to upset her. But she was taking this new lead seriously because the information represented a departure from what he'd told her before. Previously, he'd taunted her by withholding information. Now, he was giving her facts.

If Josie had been captured by this man, there was surely a chance she was still alive. Perhaps she'd had amnesia after the accident and been unable to recall her name or previous life. Anything was possible.

Katie walked into the small living room, which was modestly furnished but had a panoramic view of the St. Mary's River which ran through the town of Sault Ste. Marie, demarcating the border between the US and Canada. Katie's apartment was on the US side.

She glanced into the hall mirror as she made her way through to the kitchen to get coffee on, running a hand through her brown, shoulder-length hair and noting that her green eyes looked worried and stressed. Hardly surprising after the disaster that had played out yesterday with Leblanc.

As she waited for the coffee machine to brew, Katie acknowledged to her surprise that spending time in her place had a calming effect. The apartment was small, with light, clean, tranquil decor. With two bedrooms, a living room, and a small kitchen, it felt cozy and in the past few months, she'd come to think of it as home.

She had no family photos to put up in her house. She and her parents had been estranged since Josie's accident, despite her recent efforts to reconcile.

Last week, though, her mother had gotten in touch and asked to be kept updated on any information on the case. Katie had been stunned that her mother was reaching out. She wondered if this represented a chance that one day, they might heal the rift.

She poured coffee and returned to the living room. There, bent over her desk, Katie read through each one of the witness reports in the case that she now had in front of her. She couldn't shake the feeling she was missing something. There must be some way she could look in a different direction and find new information, but she had no idea what that was.

She'd read these same documents a hundred times, but today she resolved to go over each page more carefully and try to dredge up her memories of the neighbors and friends who'd joined the search.

She was about to study the witness reports yet again, when her phone rang.

It was her mother. The sight of that number on her screen jolted Katie.

She wasn't used to her mother calling. She didn't know what to say when she picked up. Small talk had never been her forte.

"Hi, Mom," she answered briefly.

"Katie, are you well?" Her mother sounded anxious.

"Yes, I'm good, Mom, and you?"

Her mother bypassed the niceties and got straight into the reason for the call. "Your father's gone out. I still don't want him to know I'm asking you about this. I didn't want to call you during the week because I know you must be very busy. But I wondered if there was any update?"

Katie hesitated.

Should she tell her mother the latest news? She hadn't done so yet, and wasn't sure if she should or not. She wanted to learn more before she shared it. Otherwise, it might give her mother false hope.

On the other hand, her mother might know more about who the man was, or remember him. Maybe there was more information she could provide.

"Are you any closer to finding out what happened to Josie?" her mother asked.

"I hope so, Mom." Katie tried to keep her voice steady.

"Is there anything new?" Her mother's voice was filled with hope.

"There is something, yes," she finally replied, keeping her voice low. She realized that it was comforting to be able to discuss this with someone so close to her.

"Really? What is it? Tell me."

"Last week, I visited Charles Everton in prison. He finally admitted that he saw Josie. And he said he didn't kill her. That she was unconscious on the riverbank. And he saw someone else nearby. A dark-haired man with a beard."

That was as far as she dared to go. She couldn't tell the full truth of what he'd said.

"What?" Her mother's voice was high and shocked. Katie could tell this was a massive bombshell for her. "Why didn't you tell me sooner?"

"Mom, I didn't want to call when Dad was there. Not after you asked me to keep it confidential."

"Okay. Okay." Her mother sounded as if, for a moment, she'd forgotten the complexity surrounding their circumstances.

"I don't want to get your hopes up, but I want to look into it further before I say too much. I don't want to provide false information. I'm not even sure if what he said was true, but to me, it sounded as if it might be."

"I understand," her mother said, but her voice was shaking. "I'm going to think back on who it could be."

Katie could see she'd thrown her into a state of emotional turmoil and instinctively she felt it would be unwise to say more.

She didn't want her mother to know that Everton had said the man had taken Josie. She thought that might be too much for her mother to deal with. One bombshell was enough. And there was no proof he'd done so, only Everton's word.

But her mother might know more about who this man was. So giving her the description had been the right thing to do, Katie decided.

"Thank you for telling me. I have to go now. Someone's at the door." Her mother's voice sounded brittle, and then the line went dead.

Katie put down her cell phone, feeling conflicted, wondering if she should have waited until she knew more before she shared what she had. At least the conversation had helped her understand how much anxiety her mother must have suppressed over the years, worrying without any answers, just as she herself had done.

She was about to turn back to the witness statements her phone rang again.

With thoughts of Leblanc and her mother uppermost in her mind, she grabbed it up, but found it was neither of the two.

Instead, it was Detective Scott, who headed up the cross-border task force.

"Morning, Scott," Katie said, feeling expectant about what this call might bring on a Sunday morning.

"Morning, Katie. I have a new case that's been called in."

She felt expectant as she waited to hear more. What would it bring? Already, her mind was racing ahead as she wondered where it would be based, and what it involved.

"A killer escaped from a maximum-security prison in Maine a week ago. Name of Vincent Sweeney. It looks like he may have fled north. Last night, a woman's body was found on a small uninhabited island in Nova Scotia. The body is a day or two old. She was stabbed in the back with a large, bladed weapon, which is the identical MO to one of the first murders Sweeney committed."

"Understood," Katie said, determination flaring inside her.

"There's a full-scale manhunt already under way in Maine to catch Sweeney, but with this body discovered in Nova Scotia, it's clearly got international repercussions, so we're being called in to manage the situation. We need this guy found and caught before he kills again."

"I'm glad we have the chance to get on it early," Katie agreed.

"I've tried to call Leblanc but his phone's off. Can you go and knock on his door, see if he's available? I need to organize a helicopter transfer to Halifax as soon as possible for you."

"I'll go there immediately," Katie said.

She felt a mixture of dread and apprehension that she would be confronting her case partner just a day after their blow-up.

She had no idea whether she'd be able to work with Leblanc when things were so strained, or if he was on the point of accepting the new job and quitting the task force, but she had to do her best.

A dangerous killer was at large, and a woman had already died. Every moment now counted in the quest to hunt him down.

CHAPTER THREE

After a sleepless night, Leblanc felt furious beyond words with himself as he dressed, ready for the grim and cloudy Sunday ahead. He had spent the whole of Saturday bitterly regretting his actions, and worse still, he wasn't sure how far back in time he would have to go before he stopped regretting the destructive path he'd embarked on.

Katie's words had seared into him. He'd thought they were cutting, unfair, critical.

But were they true? He uncomfortably acknowledged that there was truth in what she'd said.

He'd acted unprofessionally. In fact, she would have every right to tell Scott about his behavior and motives. He'd put his own self-interest ahead of everything. Putting personal revenge uppermost when applying for a job was highly unethical. Now he saw how far down this path he'd strayed. A lack of ethics was not a trait that an investigator should possess. The desire for personal payback should never be acted upon, especially not in such a senior position, where the incumbent should act with integrity and be fully trustworthy.

What a mad fool he'd been.

He'd been hell bent on destroying Gagnon, the person who'd made him into the monster he now acknowledged he was, who'd created the anger and pain he felt inside. He'd wanted to exact punishment, meted out by his own hand.

Now, too late, he was realizing the folly of every turn he'd taken along this twisted road.

If Scott found out about the full extent of his actions, he might be removed from the task force. He might be relieved of his position and sent home.

Sighing, Leblanc realized he had no idea what he should do to make things right.

He felt as if he was on the edge of a precipice. One wrong step, and he could be gone. His actions could already have made his future disappear.

Perhaps he was not cut out for the job, and should just walk away from it all. Briefly, the idea of making a complete break, of starting afresh in a new career in some other country, appealed.

But where would he go?

Only now, at this critical time, did he see how much his role with the task force meant to him. And his partnership with Katie. The thought of losing that tore at his heart. Why hadn't he realized earlier how much this truly meant to him?

He could tell her he'd learned his lesson and he'd do better in future. He could apologize and ask for another chance. But would she give it to him?

Leblanc glanced down at his phone, seeing with a jolt that it was turned off.

That was no good. It was a sign of how this entire debacle had affected him. An investigator always needed to keep his phone open.

He fumbled for the on switch, and after a moment, a notification popped up. Someone had called him. In fact, he had a few missed calls.

Katie?

His mind went immediately to her as he glanced down.

Yes, there were three missed calls from her and his guilt tripled as he saw them. But the most recent call hadn't been from her. It had been from Scott.

Self-blame descended.

His boss had called. There must be a case on the go. And he had been skulking around with his phone off, still licking his wounds from the confrontation with Katie yesterday, and trying not to think about the fact he had almost veered down a path that was dark and wrong.

He could still feel temptation whispering his name. Telling him that it would all be worth it, the wrong reasons, the bad decisions, would all be worthwhile if at the end he was able to look down at the lifeless body of Hugo Gagnon.

But now he felt those persuasive words were emptier than they had been. Katie's truths, spoken from the heart, had hollowed out those hopes.

Leblanc shook his head.

He would have to call Scott back and apologize sincerely for his phone being off. Most probably he should also tell him about the circumstances behind it. How much he should say, he wasn't sure. He'd been neglecting his current job, taking days off for undisclosed reasons, abusing his position, and that was unforgivable.

But at that moment, he jumped guiltily as he heard a knock on his door.

Leblanc rushed to the door and flung it open. There stood Katie.

His heart lurched at the sight of her. As he looked at her face, a chill descended. Her expression was guarded, her eyes cool and sharp. She didn't look happy to see him.

He felt a lump in his throat. He'd really screwed things up.

He wanted to tell her he had made an error, that he was going to deal with his demons and he was ready to move forward with her.

But then he decided those words might be too late. Was she here to tell him she was partnering up with someone else?

"I'm sorry," he got out. "My phone was off. I just saw Scott called."

"There's a new case landed," she said.

He blinked. "Are you on it? Are—are we on it?" he stammered.

"Do you want to be?" she asked.

Leblanc realized he didn't know. After what had happened and what he'd told her, he thought it might be better to take some time off. He needed to sort out his priorities. Top of the list was to get back to the Paris police department and tell them that after serious consideration he had decided to decline the job offer, with thanks and gratitude, and remain with the task force.

If it wasn't too late for that.

His head was a mess. Katie didn't deserve this. She didn't deserve him. But one very clear thought penetrated his confusion. He could not let her go out on a dangerous case alone. And he knew well that the cases where the task force was asked to intervene were mostly dangerous.

He could not lose her. He'd already lost one partner. Imagine if, in his search for revenge, he destroyed his own life by having Katie go out on a high-risk assignment without him to watch her back?

"Of course I do," he said. "Do you?"

He realized he felt extremely anxious waiting for her to answer. He looked at her set mouth, her narrowed eyes. He could see she was thinking hard, and desperately wanted to know what was going on in her mind.

"I do," she replied. But she didn't sound sure, and he didn't blame her for that.

He wanted to tell her he was sorry, that he'd acted like a fool, that he realized now that his behavior had been unprofessional. She needed to know that even though he might have jeopardized his career, he was still hoping for a second chance.

But he was hard pressed to get the words out. He imagined how she felt now, being on a case with a partner who'd gone behind her back and who hadn't told her the truth about his motives.

Trust was essential between investigation partners. They'd thrashed that out between them once before. Then and there, Leblanc decided that he was never going to act this way again.

In fact, his behavior had been shameful.

"We'd better go," Katie said. "There's a helicopter waiting for us."

Leblanc hesitated, looking at her, wanting to tell her what he'd learned, what he'd realized, what he wanted to take forward in the future.

But he couldn't put it into words. And he didn't have time.

"Tell me about the case," he said, grabbing his travel bag.

"We're hunting down an escaped convict who's suspected of having killed again in the past few days. The body was found last night. I'll tell you more on the way to the helicopter. It's waiting to take us to Nova Scotia."

Katie turned to lead the way and, with his stomach churning, Leblanc followed her out.

CHAPTER FOUR

The thrum of the chopper blades cut the air. Sitting next to Leblanc, Katie stared out, looking down at the Nova Scotia mainland and the multitude of large and small islands that formed a complex, jagged pattern in the indigo sea.

On this gray Sunday, the islands looked dark, their mountainous, forested shapes wreathed in cloud. An unseasonably warm few days had melted the snow, and Katie knew that on ground level, the islands were both scenic and beautiful, but as she looked down, she couldn't shake the impression they looked wintry and forbidding.

Perhaps that was because of the fugitive who was using them as his hiding place and killing ground. An evil man was lurking among these scattered islands, separated by gray, churning waters.

This was a rugged, untamed part of the world, with thousands of lakes and hundreds of rivers. The terrain was wild, with few of the islands farmed at all—in fact, Katie remembered reading that apart from the fertile lowlands, the majority of the province was unsuitable for agriculture.

This was a hard and unforgiving part of the world and it occurred to her that this convict, Vincent Sweeney, must have a reason for choosing it. It was certainly not the easiest place to flee, hide, and survive. The first two maybe, but survival was crucial.

All he had done so far was to kill. Why?

"So he escaped from prison a week ago, and he came here?" Leblanc said to her, as he read through the short briefing notes Scott had sent. He was clearly also puzzled by why the killer had chosen this area.

"Yes. Obviously, he fled over the border to try and get away from the FBI," Katie said. "Perhaps he thought that in a place with so many islands, it would be easier to hop from place to place and keep ahead of law enforcement."

"So he was last seen in New Brunswick, near the coast," Leblanc read aloud. "He robbed a convenience store and knocked out the owner but didn't kill him."

"Leaving him alive might have been unintentional. He might have meant to kill him, but just been in a hurry to get away," Katie theorized.

He was clearly on a trajectory that would take him to the islands, Katie saw, following his route on the map.

Who was Vincent Sweeney? Who was the person they were hunting? What was his background and criminal record?

Scott had helpfully summarized for them, and she read the notes out loud.

"Thirty-three years old. Convicted of multiple murders. Stabbed his boss in the back. Attacked and killed his neighbor with a pair of garden shears in the same way. Beat a driver to death in a road rage incident while on the run."

Katie never ceased to feel shocked and unsettled by the internal coldness it would take to commit crimes like these. Staring at his glowering eyes under low, dark brows, she knew that Vincent Sweeney had no respect for human life. He was a violent man who would kill using whatever means was available.

He was going to be extremely dangerous if cornered.

That meant she and Leblanc needed to have each other's back all the way on this case. Katie felt a shiver of doubt about that. Could she trust him, after yesterday's bombshell? Was he going to be fully invested in this case, or just marking time until he could move to Paris?

"Let's go over the profile again," Katie said, pushing her thoughts aside and looking over the notes she'd been compiling. "He's not a Canadian local. He was born in the US and spent most of his life there. So he's going to be in unfamiliar territory. That gives us an advantage as he's not on his home ground."

"But it makes it more difficult to predict his whereabouts, as he's not heading to anywhere he knows," Leblanc pointed out.

"True," Katie said. "We don't have a pattern for him yet. He's killed once, and he's fled along a route taking him out to the east."

"But he has managed to stay on the run for a week, despite all the FBI's efforts to find him. That suggests that he's got some survival skills, but he's got to be getting close to the end of his resources by now," Leblanc said.

"Agreed," Katie said. "He might be getting desperate. He's going to have to keep committing other crimes. Theft, robbery. He'll need food, clothes. Probably a boat. He's going to want to stay a few steps ahead of the police. Hiding out in the islands is all well and good but you need resources. Especially in this tough terrain."

"He could also be hiding out somewhere on the Nova Scotia peninsula, or Cape Breton Island," Leblanc suggested.

"True," Katie agreed.

"In any case, I feel like we're starting from a good standpoint," Leblanc said. "We know what he looks like, we know his name. We know a lot about him. There's already a manhunt under way, and the airports and border crossings are alerted to look out for him."

"And we can map his route so far, which seems to be taking him out to the most remote and isolated place he can find," she said.

The helicopter was spiraling in to land in the capital city of Halifax. Staring at the map, Katie saw it was about ten miles from the coastal village that neighbored the small island where the crime scene had been discovered.

"A teenage girl found the body after rowing out to the island at night with a friend," Leblanc said, glancing again at the report.

Katie shivered. She felt desperately sorry for the girl and could imagine what a terrifying ordeal it must have been to stumble on a corpse.

She'd been lucky the killer was not still on site. But why had he gone there in the first place, and where had he fled?

Those were questions they needed answered. And soon there would be answers, because the helicopter was coming in to land.

They touched down on the helipad, grabbed their bags, and climbed out. Katie nodded a quick thank-you to the pilot, and then they headed over to the waiting RCMP officer.

He introduced himself as Sergeant Grant Callum.

"Agent Winter and Detective Leblanc," Katie said.

"Come with me. I've got a car parked here, and there's a motorboat already waiting in Brixton, which is the small town where the witness lives."

Katie nodded. Grant Callum led the way past the buildings that housed the helicopter hangar and they climbed into the car.

As they headed out of Halifax, Katie stared curiously around her. This was the first time she'd been to Nova Scotia. At the level of the road, the terrain was even more rugged than it had appeared from the air. Callum accelerated smoothly onto the main road, and in a couple of minutes they had left the city behind and were heading southwest, through craggy, forested wilderness.

*

Fifteen minutes later, they reached the tiny town of Brixton, which was little more than two cross streets. Callum headed straight for the pier, where a small but sturdy motorboat was moored. They climbed in. The propeller churned, and the boat headed out onto the water.

Katie and Leblanc sat on the rear bench, watching as the boat made for the island which was close by and small, with a rock-scattered beach and a forested inland. The ocean was gray and churning, and the wind was strong.

Shivering, Katie pulled the hood of her windbreaker up. It was cold out here on the water, but it was strangely compelling too. She could see how lovers of the outdoors, who wanted to feed their eyes and souls with views of stark, natural beauty, would be drawn to the area.

"Here we are," Callum said, easing back on the throttle as he approached the rocky beach.

Katie could see the twisted, gnarled branches of the trees that loomed just a few yards from the shore. The sky was heavy with clouds and the wind was cold.

She hoped that on this stark, dark, uninhabited island, they might somehow find clues to the killer's whereabouts. Why this island? Was Sweeney lying low somewhere in Brixton, tiny as the town was? She didn't want to dwell on the thought, but couldn't help wondering if he might even still be hiding out among these thick trees on the island itself, invisible and unseen. They would need to watch their backs carefully as they hunted for evidence.

CHAPTER FIVE

When Katie and Leblanc arrived at the narrow, rocky beach they saw several other boats already there. Coast Guard and RCMP were on the scene, and this reassured Katie that it would be more difficult for the killer either to escape, or to strike again, if he was still on the island.

She scrambled out of the boat, treading over the rocky shore with cold surf sheeting over her shoes. The officer managing the scene hurried over to them.

"This is Detective Sergeant Jordan Shaughnessy," Callum said.

Katie nodded to Shaughnessy. Roughly the same age as her, he was a tall, brisk, capable-looking man who wore a light windbreaker and didn't seem to be feeling the cold at all.

"Agent Winter, Detective Leblanc," Shaughnessy said. "I'm glad you're going to be involved."

"Thank you," Katie said. "I'm going to need to know more about the victim."

"She's been IDed as an American tourist," Shaughnessy explained. "Name of Pauline Briggs, thirty-six years old. From Oklahoma City."

"Was she alone?" Katie asked.

"Yes, I believe she was originally going to vacation with a friend, but the friend cancelled last minute due to a family crisis, so Pauline decided to go ahead on her own. She was staying at a hotel a few miles away, on the coast."

"And how did she get here? Did she go sailing? Was there any evidence of a boat nearby, or signs of how she got here?"

Shaughnessy shook his head. "Nobody knows. The hotel said she'd been out and about a lot of the time, and they hadn't seen much of her."

"When did they realize she was missing?"

"Last night, when she hadn't checked out. She'd been missing for a day by then, they thought. At least it was that long since anyone had seen her. They tried to call her phone, but it was turned off. They then reported her missing, with a description."

"And was there a search?"

Shaughnessy made a face. "There was a search. But this time of year, tourists are already starting to arrive. We have more than a few people go missing every year. Between locals and tourists, boats capsize, people drown, people are lost but then find their way back and leave and go home without ever being reported as found. We're not sure how many actual deaths there are. There is such a huge coastline, and so many islands, that you can never fully search it."

Katie nodded, appreciating the complexity of this challenge. She saw Leblanc was looking serious as he took it in.

"But this was definitely a murder?"

"Without a doubt. She was stabbed in the back, repeatedly, with a sharp, bladed weapon. She was fully dressed. Stabbed right through her shirt and a thick windbreaker. So it must have been a heavy weapon, used with force. Possibly something like a fishing spear, the coroner has theorized."

"Were there any other signs of a struggle? Was she bruised, scratched, any other injuries?"

"She had a scratch on her face which might have been from a low-hanging branch. Apart from that, no other injuries."

That interested Katie as it showed that the woman must have been either surprised by the killer, or else overpowered very efficiently, either by being subdued or threatened. She hadn't struggled for her life and broken away, or there would surely be more signs of a fight. Had she known she was on a boat with a killer? Or had the killer followed her here? What exactly had played out?

The answers were elusive in the growing darkness.

"Did she have any ID or money on her? Her phone, perhaps?" Katie asked.

"No. There was no sign of her purse anywhere, nor any items that might have fallen out of a purse, such as coins. If she dropped it when she fled, the killer must have picked it up."

"Was the body moved?" Katie asked. "Does the coroner think she was killed where she fell, or could the killer have transported her?"

"No evidence that it was moved. She must have been killed as she fled, given that the wounds are from behind. Let me take you to the scene. It's not far."

Katie could already see the yellow tape flapping in the breezy woods. They paced toward it.

"The girl who found the body, Emily Daly, literally stumbled over it in the dark," Shaughnessy said solemnly.

Standing on the spot where it happened, Katie guessed that the victim had fled. What other reason would there be to run a few yards along this narrow, overgrown path, before being struck from behind?

Katie felt deeply sorry for a life that had ended in such a brutal way, while fleeing in terror. Even when the bodies had been removed, seeing the sights of the scene always affected her this way. She knew a hard but necessary part of being a good investigator was being able to see what the victim had seen, and feel what the victim had felt.

The worst part was having to do the same through the killer's eyes.

Katie was beginning to piece together what must have happened. The killer must surely have transported the woman here, alive, because if she'd been with anyone else, there would either be a witness or another body. Who knew if she was aware of her danger or not, at that stage? They reached the island, he pursued her, and he killed her.

"Are there any other bodies?" she asked.

"We've searched the perimeter, and there are none on the beach or near the outskirts of the woods. We're still checking the interior, but it's very overgrown."

"So the killer most likely used a boat to bring her here alone. Or he hid away on a boat she personally hired," she guessed.

"That's what must have happened. She didn't hire any boat through the hotel, so we can't take that lead any further."

"Were there any other tourist boats in the area? Anyone who reported seeing anything unusual?"

Shaughnessy shook his head. "Lots of boat traffic in the wider area, but it's impossible to track down who was where, given the delay between the murder and the body being found. We're trying to get a picture of what happened the day before yesterday, but we don't even have a specific time of day."

"Have you circulated Sweeney's description to all the boat rental companies?"

"Yes. We've circulated it as widely as possible. We've asked people to come forward if they have seen anyone who even vaguely resembles him. We've got it out in the media and we've notified all the hotels. But so far, we have no hits. There have been two false leads called in, but apart from that, nothing."

"Any evidence of where on this island they would have moored the boat?" Leblanc asked.

He'd been silent up till now, but Katie was relieved to see that he was clearly thinking as hard about this puzzle as she was.

"Unfortunately, this shoreline is so rocky, there are no signs of where they might have come to shore."

Given the intensive search that had been conducted around the island's coast, Katie concluded that the absence of any boat indicated that the killer was no longer here, and that he had sailed away after the kill.

"Have you got any teams out, searching boats on the water, looking for any evidence of the killer? Any other sightings of Sweeney? Any other robberies or violent crimes that might be linked?"

"We are working on the reports," Shaughnessy said. "But it's difficult to police every boat. We have patrols, but there are so many small boats and so few of us. Plus, so many people are on the water for the purpose of fishing. So finding a weapon like that in a boat is not going to be overly helpful to us. What I can tell you is that there were no robberies recently reported in this town, and no stolen boats."

"The girl who found the body," Katie said. "She's been debriefed?"

"Yes. She and her friend were both interviewed," Shaughnessy said. "They're both sixteen years old. Emily is being sent for counseling, to help her deal with it."

"We'd like to speak to her. Is that possible?"

"Of course. She's at home. She's very traumatized, but I'm sure she'll gladly help you with a direct interview. She's very anxious to find out who did it, because the island is so close to her house."

Katie could understand her worry. She looked out over the water, at the waves tossing whitecaps onto the mainland shore. The breeze was strong.

There was no more to be picked up from the crime scene. It was a cold, lonely, and strangely sad place. Katie hoped that the next piece of the puzzle, interviewing the witness who found the body, might be able to provide further insight. Sometimes people remembered things after the fact that hadn't seemed important at the time, or which had been blocked out by trauma.

"Let's see if Emily remembers any helpful details," she said.

CHAPTER SIX

Leblanc felt weighed down with discouragement as he approached the whitewashed house where Emily Daly lived. He walked together with Katie and Officer Callum, who'd transported them back to the mainland. The small home, about thirty yards from the beach, was set on a rocky slope, under a fringe of dark, twisted trees.

Already, the light was failing, and afternoon was darkening to a grim, cloudy evening. Lights were on in the house, casting a warm, golden aura into the growing dark.

This was going to be a tough case. The cliché *needle in a haystack* rang in his mind. That was what it felt like, trying to follow the trail of one desperate and violent convict in this complicated network of islands and seas.

"I hope we can find answers here," he muttered.

Katie nodded in a way that told him she hoped exactly the same, and had all the same misgivings he did.

He felt grateful that they were able to work together after the debacle of yesterday morning.

More and more, thanks to her words, he was realizing how he'd taken temporary leave of his senses by considering the Paris post. Or perhaps his sanity.

Alone, isolated, not communicating his feelings, he'd allowed his thoughts to fester, allowed grief and revenge to consume him.

Pushing the stark reality of his predicament aside, he walked up and knocked on the door.

A woman in her forties answered it, looking pale and shocked. She had dark blond hair which looked as if it had frizzed up in the damp conditions, and bright blue eyes.

"Oh, good evening, Officer, you're here again? Is there any news?" she asked Callum, before glancing curiously at Leblanc and Katie.

"These are Agent Winter and Detective Leblanc from the cross-border task force," Callum said. "It's a special unit that investigates serious crimes. Can we speak to Emily again?"

"Sure, of course. Come in."

She led them through to a small living room, where a fire burned brightly in the fireplace. There, a young girl sat on a sofa, watching TV. She looked up when they entered.

She had her mother's hair and eyes, but was fairer, more delicate and small boned. She looked younger than sixteen, and her red eyes showed she'd clearly been crying. Even so, as soon as they walked in, she gathered herself together, turned off the TV, and stood up to greet them.

"Hi, are you detectives?" she asked in a small voice.

Leblanc let Katie speak, knowing her sympathetic manner would do more to put this troubled girl at ease.

"Yes. We'd like to ask you a few questions, Emily."

He and Katie sat down side by side on the neat, plaid couch. Her mother stood near the door, looking nervous and worried. Callum's phone rang, and, with a quick nod of apology, he headed out to take the call.

"Thank you for being so brave and helpful," Katie said to Emily. "It's not easy, revisiting what happened and going through it all again."

"I'm trying my best to cope with it all," Emily said.

"Can you tell me about the evening? What happened?"

"My friend Sandi decided we should sail to the island on a dare. She had some beers." Emily glanced uneasily at her mother.

"We're not angry, honey," her mother said. "Honestly, we are just so glad you are still alive and safe."

Emily sighed. "We were not supposed to be out at night and drinking. We took my dad's rowboat across to the island. It was dark, and I felt spooked. I knew what we were doing was wrong."

"Go on."

"We lost an oar just before we reached it. The sea was rough," Emily remembered. "We were stuck there and I felt very panicky."

"Did you see or hear anything that made you afraid?" Katie asked.

"I have a very strong imagination, or so my mom says. So I was thinking I saw people from even before we arrived. But the truth was that I don't think there was anything at all. It was just me being spooked."

"Go on," Katie encouraged.

"We got there and I was already thinking I should call my folks, that something was wrong. It was cold and I—I needed to pee, so I went into the woods. I literally fell over her. I mean, I couldn't believe it. I stumbled and fell and when I turned the flashlight on, there was a body. You could see she'd been killed. She was lying on her side, wearing this blue windbreaker, and there was blood all over the back of it."

"What happened then?" Katie asked.

"I screamed and screamed. I, like, totally panicked. Then my friend Sandi came running to see what was wrong. She told me not to scream. She said if anyone was still here, they'd hear us. She said we should go and hide behind a rock until help came."

Leblanc felt a brief flash of admiration. Though clearly a troublemaker, Sandi was a quick thinker.

"What did you do?" he asked.

"We called my folks, like, immediately after we'd hidden. We told them what had happened and they said they would call the police and Coast Guard. My dad was here in our speedboat within ten minutes. He was totally panicked and he was mad at us. The police were here soon afterward. We had to walk where it had happened and show them. Then they let us go home."

"Did you see anything along the way going back?" Katie asked.

"No. We had a police boat riding alongside us. I wasn't looking but my dad said there was nothing to be seen."

She spoke in a small voice, twisting her fingers nervously.

"We're not mad, honey," her mother repeated. "Your dad was just worried. I mean, I can't believe there is a killer at large here. Who would do such a thing? Last time the police were here, they mentioned it might be an escaped convict. Has he been caught?"

"No. We're hunting for him and have as many resources as possible allocated to this," Katie said firmly.

"The manhunt is large scale," Callum said, walking back in. "We're allocating all the resources we can. RCMP, Coast Guard, and volunteers and police reservists. We have more than a hundred people combing the area now. We're using two helicopters and three drones, one of which is donated. Truly, everyone in this area is on the alert and getting involved."

"I hope you catch him soon. We can't sleep at night knowing this. We don't feel safe."

"I'm going to ask our local patrols to pay special attention to this area of the coast," Callum said.

Leblanc nodded, appreciating the efforts that the community was making, and feeling deeply sympathetic to their plight. But it was clear that there was no new information to be had from this witness.

"Thank you for your time," he said after glancing at Katie.

They headed outside.

"What would you like to do now?" Callum asked. "We can make a vehicle available to you if you need one, and you are welcome to base yourself in the closest RCMP department here in Halifax."

Katie moved a few steps away to discuss the options, and Leblanc followed.

"What do you say we join the search?" he asked. "That seems to be where the biggest need is."

He saw she was looking doubtful and pushed his case.

"We are experienced. We have been in a similar situation. I'm sure they'd welcome our knowledge, as well as extra feet on the ground."

"I feel differently," she said.

"What do you think we should do?" he asked.

"I want to look more closely at the victim's movements," she said.

"Why's that?" Leblanc asked, knowing Emily's answer would provide a valuable perspective.

"I don't feel this happened randomly. It doesn't make sense. A woman on her own, staying in a hotel? How did she get miles away from where she was on a boat? There are way too many unanswered questions here. Was she forced to get on the boat and if so how was she approached? The hotel doesn't know, so how did this all happen? Did the killer—we'll assume it's Sweeney—act normal, fitting in with the crowds? Was he pretending to work for a boat rental company? Did he befriend her?"

Leblanc nodded.

"I see what you're saying," he said. "Those are all good questions."

"I think that, somehow, she was hunted. And we need to try and work out how it happened. Where it happened. We need to get better parameters on Sweeney's mindset, how he's approaching her, and the resources he has available. I'd like to spend a while profiling him. I think that will get us further than heading out on a search."

Leblanc nodded. "I think you're right. We have space available to use at the police department. We might find information that can make the picture clearer."

CHAPTER SEVEN

Maureen Eagle trod over the dark terrain, her ankle twisting as she stepped on a rock, invisible in the shadowy evening.

"Okay there?" Gideon, her neighbor, asked.

"Yes, I'm good," she replied, redirecting the beam of her flashlight so it lit exactly where she walked.

Somewhere out here was a killer. And she had volunteered to be part of the search party, led by a member of the Canadian Coast Guard, that was combing the small, uninhabited islands near their home in western Nova Scotia.

The search had begun at midday, and Maureen had been told to report to a rendezvous point near the local pier, where two Coast Guard boats had been waiting to take them out.

Maureen was wearing old-fashioned laced-up rubber boots and a waterproof jacket that was a bit too big, because it belonged to her husband, Neil. She had in her hand a large, powerful Maglite that her friend Tammy had lent her.

She was glad to be part of the search team; it had been a horrible day after the news had broken. Their community was in a panic. Maureen had two daughters in their twenties, and she couldn't bear the thought of them being targeted.

So she was heading out on this rather terrifying search, in the hope that their neighborhood would end up being safer.

Safer for her, and her husband, who couldn't join the search party because he was a nurse who was on shift at this time. For their daughters and their boyfriends.

For everyone who didn't deserve to die at the hands of this escaped convict.

She felt sick as she thought about what he could do to her daughters. Rather than thinking about that, she focused on the beam of light in front of her as her breath steamed in the chilly air.

This was the last thing she would have imagined doing. She was a suburban woman. A mother who had raised her kids, and who today worked part time at the local veterinary clinic.

She had never imagined that she would be out here, hunting a killer. In the dark, on a fairly large, but uninhabited island she'd never visited. It was a rough, craggy place. She'd heard an owl hoot as she arrived, and heard rustling from the undergrowth that she guessed meant that an animal was lurking there.

Maureen didn't know what animals might lurk on this large, wild island. Never had she imagined there would be a killer to hunt just a few miles from her home.

But here they were. And she was determined to do whatever it took to help find him. At the moment, their best option seemed to be to search the islands to see if there were any clues to where the killer was hiding out, as well as where he had been.

She heard the whip-whip of chopper blades overhead. At this time, it was oddly reassuring. But at the same time, her mind was turning over and over with the puzzle pieces of this terrible crime.

Maureen was trying to work out how the killer had managed to capture and abduct an innocent tourist. How had he gotten this woman onto a boat? He surely must have done that to take her across the sea. Did he have a boat himself? Was it a stolen boat?

Was he an experienced sailor? She knew that these questions were important. But she had no idea of the answers, and in fact couldn't bear to think of how the scene might have played out. The whole thing shook her to the core.

She saw a small path in the distance, and she moved toward it as the group fanned out. "We can't go much further in the dark," the officer in charge called. "Let's give it ten more minutes, and then wrap up and go back to the boats."

Feeling relieved that nightfall was bringing an end to this long day of searching, Maureen walked carefully along the track, aware of the lights of the other searchers that were now a few yards away on either side of her.

It had been a weird day, with the helicopters overhead, and the Coast Guard boats, and the search parties comprised of people all over the town. The whole community was involved in the hunt. Everyone was on edge. She knew that her daughters were scared.

Listening out, Maureen heard the canopy of a large tree groaning in the darkness, over her head. And she heard a soft rustling of leaves, but didn't see anything. The only other noise was the scrunching of footsteps from the other searchers. Through the overgrowth she could see their lights faintly coming and going.

She shone her flashlight into the nearby bushes, wary of animals. Then she focused on the path again, worried about the uneven terrain. She didn't want to fall into a ditch in the dark and hurt herself badly, or worse.

And then she heard something that made her stop in her tracks.

Coming from the thick knot of bushes just off the path, she heard a weird ripping, tearing noise she couldn't identify at all. But for some reason it chilled her blood. It wasn't a nice sound. It was a threatening, feral sound.

She moved her light slowly, watching as the beam reflected off something. There was movement there. Her heart leaped into her mouth and all the dangers of her mission came back to her in a rush.

This was risky! Anything could be waiting ahead. It couldn't be a bear, or anything like that, could it?

She'd been told long ago there were bears on the island, but they tended to be shy and they liked to stay away from people. But she didn't know if that was true. Surely it couldn't be? That must be an old wives' tale.

Maureen froze, staring, trying to work out what the pattern of light and shade meant, because she didn't want to be an alarmist and cause the whole search party to grind to a stop because of an innocent creature going about its business. She had absolutely resolved that she was not going to be the person to do that.

For a moment, she felt a surge of self-doubt. Maybe she wasn't up to this. Maybe she didn't actually want to be out here in the dark hunting a killer after all. Because what if it wasn't an animal under those bushes but the killer himself, crawling deeper in to hide?

And at that exact moment, there was a loud rustling of leaves, and the sound of something crashing through the undergrowth.

Maureen couldn't help it. She let out a shriek of alarm.

Instantly, she heard concerned cries and shouts from around her. Flashlight beams swung in her direction as the search party began to converge.

But as she shone the light, it reflected off a pair of gleaming eyes as they peered at her from the darkness.

As it bolted, lean and lithe, she saw the distinctive feline shape of a bobcat.

Just a cat. Her nerve had broken and now she'd completely disrupted the entire search with that scream. She'd thrown a serious wrench in the works. Now they might miss the killer because they were all coming to rescue her from a harmless wild cat that had just been having its dinner.

"It's all right," she called, feeling her face flame. "False alarm, guys. False alarm. It was just a cat. It was in here."

She shone the flashlight at the bushes where it had been, as Gideon bashed through the undergrowth and rushed up to her in concern.

"Just a cat," she repeated.

It had been eating something. Ripping meat from bones. But then, with a chill, Maureen wondered what that something had been. Because it had sounded big, too. Big enough to need to be torn apart by what was, definitely, a sizeable cat.

She shone the beam deeper into the bushes. It was then that she saw it.

A hand. Just a hand. Distinctive, unmistakable, icy pale streaked with dark rust.

A human hand. A dead, bloody, human hand.

For a moment, she thought she was going to faint, and she reached out, grabbing Gideon's arm, thankful that he was there, aiming his own flashlight at the bushes in horror.

"Quickly! Come quickly!" he yelled, which was just as well because Maureen could no longer speak. She felt like she was going to throw up.

Never had she thought or dreamed she'd actually be looking at such a thing. But she stared, as if hypnotized, unable to tear her gaze away as thoughts raced through her mind.

The killer had struck again, right here, on the exact path she'd chosen to walk.

Maureen knew only too well what that meant. This was a serial killer, and that meant the danger had just compounded a hundredfold.

Every person in their wider community was now in danger.

CHAPTER EIGHT

Huddled at a desk in the corner of the small back room of the Halifax police precinct, Katie went over the facts of what they had with Leblanc.

"The killer has either stolen a boat, bought a boat, or is somehow using a boat."

Leblanc nodded. "He has to have been mobile to have taken that victim from the hotel, or from wherever she was near the hotel, to that island."

The first question was how the killer had obtained the means to do that.

Katie frowned, looking at the wall, whitewashed and papered with notices, and the darkened window beyond, without really seeing it. The heater rattled behind them, a noise she barely noticed as she puzzled over the logistics.

Had he stolen just one boat, the theft of which had not yet been picked up? Was he stealing multiple boats, using them and dumping them?

Had he stolen a boat and killed the owner, therefore covering his tracks for longer?

Or was he using the boat of someone who was unaware that they had loaned it to a killer?

Callum had told her they were running checks on boats all over Nova Scotia that had been reported stolen over the past week. There weren't many of them though. Only a couple of thefts were in the window period when the escaped convict could have picked them up.

Katie knew how important it was to try and work out the logistics of this. They needed to follow the trail.

"Then the next question is how he picked up the victim," Katie mused. "What would it have taken for a woman on her own to go out in a boat with a killer?"

Had she been threatened? Had the killer used a gun to threaten her? But if so why hadn't he killed with a gun—or in his twisted mind, did he prefer a blade?

"It's bothering me that Sweeney is not a safe-looking person," Leblanc said. "He is brutal, threatening in appearance. He has visible prison tattoos on his neck and hands which have been noted in the police alerts. Did he manage to turn on the charm, change his look? Wear gloves or a scarf? How exactly did he lure a woman, alone, out on a boat?"

"Could he have asked for help, fooled her into wanting to help somehow?" Katie suggested. "Played vulnerable, lied to her, created a sob story?"

"We can't rule that out," Leblanc agreed.

There was another possibility, one that had occurred to her and that she knew they must keep in mind.

That was the fact that the escaped convict might not have committed these crimes. They could be dealing with two separate individuals if a different serial killer had coincidentally embarked on a spree at the same time. It was an outside chance but she knew it was one they had to consider.

But, as she was grappling with this possibility, the phone rang. She grabbed it up.

"Agent Winter, it's Callum here. We have a new development in the case."

"What's that?" Katie said, switching the phone to speaker, feeling her adrenaline spike.

"We have discovered another victim. A search party has just turned up the body of a man on one of the islands. Undoubtedly, he's been killed the same way, with fatal stab wounds inflicted from behind."

She and Leblanc jumped up as one.

"Where is this? How can we get there?" she asked.

"It's a couple of miles away, to the southwest of the mainland. I'm going to drive past the police department right now. We can go to the closest harbor and take a speedboat out there," Callum said.

Katie stared at Leblanc, feeling extremely concerned by this latest development. A second kill was something she'd dreaded. Her only hope was that this body could somehow provide them with new information to hunt this murderer down.

*

An hour later, they arrived at the island. The speedboat had cut through the cold water, taking them a surprisingly long way from

Halifax harbor to a dark and rocky beach somewhere out in the cold sea. In the darkness, Katie felt disoriented. She had renewed respect for the civilians who had been working in their groups up until night fell in these cold, bleak conditions.

As Callum moored the boat next to three other vessels already on site, Katie saw the bright glare of spotlights a couple of hundred yards inland, indicating that the scene was already being attended to.

She shivered. There was something very spooky about these locations on deserted islands. The wind was even stronger here, blowing up the beach.

On shore, their feet splashed through shallow water as they moved toward the two RCMP officers standing guard near the boats.

Shaughnessy hurried over to them, looking stressed.

"The body was found in the bushes, near one of the tracks leading into the woods. It's fairly close to one of the natural harbors on this island. Come with me, and I'll show you. It's a little way up the hill here."

Katie walked behind him, up the hill and along the narrow, winding track, until she saw the glare of spotlights ahead. There, three people were working inside the crime scene tape that had been strung across the path. They had white plastic overalls on, Katie saw. Already, the body was being examined.

"Who is it? Do you have an ID yet?" Katie asked Shaughnessy.

"Yes. The victim had ID in his wallet, which was still in his coat pocket. He's Michael Bancroft, from Ohio. Age forty-eight. He's a tourist here, and was reported missing four days ago. His wife and daughter are still here."

"Four days?" Katie asked, feeling surprised. "So he's an earlier victim?"

"Does that timeline fit in with the details of Sweeney's escape?" Leblanc asked immediately.

"It does, just, based on the earlier sighting. He must have killed this victim soon after arriving here."

So he'd reached Nova Scotia and embarked on a killing spree, Katie guessed.

"Are there any clues on the body? Any defensive wounds?"

The pathologist examining Bancroft's corpse glanced around. He was a middle-aged man, with dark hair under his plastic head covering.

"Without a doubt, the deep wounds inflicted from behind were fatal. Beyond that, it's difficult to tell. Out here, when it's not freezing, we get almost immediate damage to bodies because of the amount of small wildlife, especially on these remote and uninhabited islands. This man's face and hands in particular have already been scavenged. After a few days there's often not much left apart from clothing and bones. The postmortem may tell us more."

"Was he killed on site?" Leblanc asked.

"I would say so, yes, based on what I've seen so far. I can't be totally sure, given the time that's elapsed, but the condition and placement of the body are pointing to it."

Katie thought about that. Two victims. Both American tourists. Both on their own at the time of the killings. Both taken to a small, remote island and murdered there.

The killer didn't seem to have a preference for gender or age. He'd killed one younger woman and one middle-aged man. But he was clearly targeting people alone. Somehow, he was getting them on boats and transporting them out to the remote islands where he preferred to kill.

A lot of questions were swirling in her head. Why did he take them out to islands? What was it about these that he favored? What was it about the islands that appealed to him?

Was he taking advantage of sites where he knew he could dispose of the body, where it would hopefully not be found? If so, why? Why not kill on the mainland and dump the body there?

The other worrying thing was that these kills had occurred within a couple of days of each other. This killer was working on a fast interval and that meant a higher level of danger and risk.

As well as being brutal and violent, the killer was obviously intelligent and cunning. He was someone who thought ahead and planned his actions.

Katie turned away from the disturbing sight of the corpse.

"We need to find out if there's any information on Bancroft's movements prior to his death. Any activities he was planning on doing, or places he was going to. He might have made reservations somewhere, or mentioned where he was headed."

Leblanc nodded. "I hope his family can tell us more."

CHAPTER NINE

This was Katie's least favorite part of an investigation, she thought grimly as she climbed out of the police car loaned to them by Callum. Speaking to traumatized, recently bereaved relatives brought all her own demons raging to the surface. The trauma, fear, guilt, and anguish she'd experienced after Josie's accident had never left her. It had just been deeply suppressed.

She approached the beachfront hotel in Halifax where the Bancrofts were saying, feeling as if both her feet and her heart were filled with lead.

They walked into the lobby, which was decked out in an elegant, colonial style with paneled walls, large leather couches, and polished wooden tables.

"We're here to see the Bancrofts," Katie said, and the receptionist's smile instantly vanished.

"This is so terrible. So terrible! Anna and Heather, her daughter, are in room two, up the stairs to your right."

Katie and Leblanc walked up the stairs and headed to room two.

The door was ajar. Tapping on it before opening it wider, she found Michael Bancroft's wife and daughter sitting on the bed, huddled together. They looked up as they entered. Both of them were red-eyed, tear-stained, and clearly distressed.

Katie felt her heart constrict and her throat tighten up.

"I'm Agent Winter, and this is Agent Leblanc. We're working with the RCMP on this case. We're so very sorry for your loss."

Anna Bancroft was a small, dark-haired woman who looked to be in her late thirties. She was dressed in a cream-colored tracksuit. Her face, pale and drawn, was framed by straight shoulder-length black hair. A pair of small, dark-rimmed glasses gave her a studious look. Beside her, her daughter, Heather, with long brown hair and big dark eyes, sat with a blank, expressionless gaze.

"I can't believe this. Can't." Anna shook her head.

She and Leblanc sat on the two wooden chairs at the desk, opposite the Bancrofts.

"Can you explain what happened on the day your husband disappeared?" Katie asked gently.

"It was Wednesday. Heather and I wanted to do some shopping. Mike didn't want to come along so he went out on his own."

"Do you know where?" Katie asked.

Anna shook her head. "We headed out in the afternoon, at around two p.m. We figured he'd find a nearby sports bar and hang out for a while. But he wasn't back when we returned to the hotel, and when we called him, his phone was off. We waited a couple of hours, wondering if his battery had died or there was a reason why he was out of communication. But then we decided we should report him missing."

"We phoned around all the hospitals," Heather added in a small voice.

"Yes. I thought—well—my first thought was that he'd been in a car accident, maybe taken a cab somewhere and had an accident. My second thought was that he'd taken a boat out for a sail. It was a fine day and I remember the harbor was quite busy. But the police told me they did check and ask around at the harbor, and he didn't rent a boat himself."

"Did Michael enjoy any other outdoor sports?" Leblanc asked. Katie guessed he was trying to rule out any other scenarios where he might have been abducted.

Anna shook her head. "He enjoyed being on a boat, but other than that, no. He liked to go to the gym. He was more of a gym person than a hiker." She drew in a deep, shaking breath. "I can't believe he's gone."

"Do you know which direction he was planning on going?"

"No. I don't have a clue."

"Was he familiar with the island?"

"Not at all. We arrived here a week ago and it was the first time here for all of us."

"Were there any other places he liked to go when he was here?"

"Just the gym, the restaurants, and a few bars in town. That's it."

"Did he meet anyone while he was on the island?" Leblanc asked. "Anyone he might have befriended, any tourist or local that he told you he was spending time with?"

"No. Apart from the one mutual friend we visited the day after we arrived."

The daughter, Heather, shook her head.

"I can't think of anyone either."

"I need you to look at this photo for me, please. Did you see this man at all during your stay, near the hotel or at the harbor or even on the street? Is he familiar to you?" Katie got out her iPad and showed Anna and Heather the picture of Sweeney.

"No. I don't recognize him at all. I didn't see him, that I know of."

Heather also shook her head.

Katie knew the lack of information was going to make things difficult. If a tourist wanted to go for a walk, there were hundreds of trails to choose from. If he wanted to go for a sail or a ride on a boat, there was a maze of waterways to navigate through. It seemed that Bancroft had simply left his wife and daughter to go shopping, gone out on his own, and never returned.

"Did you go on any other boat trips while you have been here?" she tried.

"Just one," Anna said. "We went out on the boat once. That's when we went to a few of the islands."

"Who organized that trip?"

"It was the mutual friend of ours I mentioned to you, Barbara, who lives outside Halifax. She owns a boat and one of our reasons for coming here was to go out on the water with her, and go out for dinner afterward. We did that on Tuesday."

"Can you tell us where you went on that trip?"

"It was to a few of the islands. Probably within a couple of miles of the main harbor. We had a hike on one of them and sailed around the others."

Katie nodded. That was a dead end, too.

"I'm sorry," Anna said, looking up at her. "I know you're doing your job, but I don't think I can cope any more now. I still can't believe it's real. He's not gone. This is just a dream, a nightmare."

Katie felt helpless.

"Thank you so much for answering the questions," she said. She got up and quietly left, feeling wrung out after the short interview as she headed downstairs and out of the hotel.

"That's the worst part of this job, you know," she said to Leblanc as they walked outside into the windy, drizzly night. "Not the violence, the horror of the things you see, it's the fact that you're completely helpless, and you know that the families are going to be devastated no matter what you find out."

"I agree with you. But that's why we have to do what we do, though," Leblanc said. "At least we can make sure that we do find out what happened. We can try to make sure that there aren't any more tragedies like this."

"I hope so," Katie said, feeling a sense of dread. They weren't anywhere close to discovering the killer's whereabouts.

However, the one thing they did know now, based on his pattern, was that he was killing on small, uninhabited islands. That was a definite trend they could identify and it could guide them in the areas they needed to focus.

"He's got hold of a boat. He's hiding it somewhere. Then, somehow luring people on their own, out onto that boat. And he's taking them to uninhabited locations to kill them," Leblanc summarized. "That sounds to me as if he's giving them a sob story. Come help me. Something like that."

"Yes, that does make sense. Perhaps he's using those islands as a hiding place," Katie suggested. "He's going to the larger towns on the mainland. Picking up a victim who's a tourist. Killing and then hiding out again. So perhaps he has a base somewhere. Or at any rate, a tent and provisions."

"Yes. That would work, for him to avoid being picked up or noticed," Leblanc agreed.

"We must tell Callum and Shaughnessy that the search and surveillance must focus on the smaller islands," Katie resolved. "I know there are hundreds of them, but at least it gives us a better chance of finding the killer, and any evidence he might leave behind."

"And what about the mainland?" Leblanc asked.

"We need to look into that. I think it would be worthwhile to look into any reports of strange or suspicious activity in the area. Any unusual crimes. He might have made a failed attempt to abduct somebody. Or robbed a store, seeking money or supplies. There might be people out there who got away from him alive, but don't know they have actually seem him."

Katie felt encouraged by the thought. They might be able to discover some missing pieces. If they could find an actual robbery victim, it could provide them with more information. What had the killer said to lure them? What was his appearance? What had he done to them? If he'd fled, where had he gone? This could lead them to uncover more about him.

"We need to go to the police department and have a search for recent crimes." Leblanc, too, sounded more positive about this new angle.

CHAPTER TEN

"I feel sure this killer must be making frequent trips to the mainland, searching for targets," Katie muttered as she pored over the police records, squashed up next to Leblanc at the small back office desk of the Halifax police department.

"I still think he's based here. In fact, I'm sure of it," Leblanc said.

"Why's that?" Katie asked.

"Those small islands are tough places to survive. Some of them are so small they don't even have fresh water. They're rocky and inhospitable. To be there, he'd have to bring water, warmth, food. A means of cooking for when the wood's wet. Shelter."

Leblanc glanced out the windows. As it was growing dark, rain was spattering the glass.

"You're right," Katie said. "They're not easy places to hide out. And he'd have to hide his boat. Which must be big enough to sail a fair distance. That last body was on an island a couple of miles from the mainland. How would you manage a rowboat? Especially with another person inside?"

"Exactly. It's a far distance, and if you're rowing, you can't be threatening a suspect as well. So if there was a boat it would have to be motorized. That means he'd need fuel."

The logistics were definitely a factor that would allow them to narrow down the suspect's movements and whereabouts, Katie realized.

Katie felt heartened that they had clearer parameters in place to start the search for relevant crimes that Sweeney could have committed.

They both logged into the database and began searching for recent reports of crimes that might fit the modus operandi and needs of this dangerous escaped convict. Katie scrolled through, speed-reading intently so as not to miss a detail.

Burglaries were first on the list, but she didn't think that Sweeney would be looking for a big-screen TV or a laptop. He was so recently arrived in Nova Scotia. He would surely not have a fence to sell the items through, or an established chain of contacts set up to move them on. And burglary was very different from murder. She instinctively felt they needed to be on the lookout for a more violent crime. Face to face. Robbery. Assault.

Just a couple of screens on, something jumped out at her and she stopped scrolling, reading more carefully.

"Here's something interesting," she said.

"What is it?" Leblanc asked.

"It's an attempted carjacking. It took place an hour ago, near one of the motorboat rental companies in Halifax. It's only just gone up on the system. The perpetrator smashed the car window and tried to assault the driver and pull him out. He grabbed his wallet and fled. Those are all the details so far, and the victim's name and address are recorded also."

"That sounds like a possibility," Leblanc said. "Why would Sweeney need a vehicle?"

"He might never have intended to take the car, but have been after the wallet only. The violence fits his style. He'd drag someone out just to intimidate them, I think."

"And he'd be after cash, for sure," Leblanc agreed.

"I think we should find out more about it," she said. "The level of violence makes me think we need to look into it. It's very recent, unusual for the area, and what was stolen matches up to what Sweeney would need."

"There's no description of the perpetrator. Just the initial report of the crime. So we need to find out if his appearance matches up to Sweeney's," Leblanc said.

When it was fully dark, she knew the searches would be called off. That would surely be any minute now. It was too dangerous out there at night, in many ways. Their window of time to find Sweeney was shortening. Katie knew that it was important to urgently pursue every lead.

At that moment, Katie's phone rang.

"Hello, Agent Winter. Callum here."

"Is there any news?" Katie felt her heart skip.

"We flushed out a possible suspect on one of the searches a couple of minutes ago. It's on a small island to the south. The man seems to have been hiding out on the island, and bolted into a thickly wooded area. The police are about to concentrate their efforts where he ran, but I wondered if one or both of you would like to come along. If you do, I'll send you the coordinates for where I have a motorboat waiting."

“Of course,” Katie said. “We’ve picked up a possible lead on a crime scene in Halifax, so we’ll probably split up and follow the two separately. One of us will be with you in five minutes.”

“Sounds good. See you soon.”

As Katie ended the call, she felt encouraged. From having no possible directions five minutes ago, they now had two different leads that both sounded worth following.

“If we have two leads, let’s follow both,” Leblanc agreed. “That way we don’t lose out on the element of speed, if the carjacker does prove to be Sweeney. We need to try and catch him fast, seeing this was so recent.”

“True. So who’s going in which direction?” Katie asked.

“I’ll go and follow up the lead on the island,” Leblanc said.

Katie knew this was probably the more dangerous option. She would have volunteered to take it, too. But Leblanc had asked first, and she could see he was desperate to redeem himself after yesterday morning’s debacle back in Sault Ste. Marie, which seemed to be a lifetime ago.

“Okay,” she said, deciding not to argue this. “I’ll follow up the carjacking as soon as I’ve dropped you off where Callum’s waiting.”

As they hurried across the police station and through the front doors, rain was thrashing the paving blocks and bouncing up into the air.

Katie pulled her jacket closed.

“This weather is not ideal,” she noted. “It’s going to be impossible to search if this rain gets worse.”

“We’ll have him by tonight, I know it.” Leblanc sounded firm.

“I hope so,” Katie said.

Wrapping their jackets more tightly around themselves, they rushed to the car and jumped in. Katie started it up and swerved out of the parking lot and into the traffic, which was moving steadily through the watery streets.

“Here’s the coordinates for where Callum’s waiting,” Leblanc said, checking his phone. “Turn right at the next crossroad, and then drive all the way down to the bottom of the road.”

With the tires hissing on the wet blacktop, Katie followed the route. She drove in silence, concentrating on the road, the windshield wipers flicking away the rain.

“There it is,” Leblanc said. “That’s Callum, waiting there.”

As Katie stopped the car, she saw him standing, swathed in a waterproof jacket, by the pier. Beyond him, the police motorboat waited. It was going to be a cold ride, and she knew that anything might happen when Leblanc reached the island. A cornered fugitive was likely to be dangerous. Leblanc had been badly injured in similar circumstances in the past.

Her own search might lead nowhere but it was still important to see if the carjacker could possibly be tracked down.

"I'll get out here. Good luck," Leblanc said, with a wan smile.

"You need it more than me," Katie said. "Be careful, Leblanc, please."

"And you, too," Leblanc said. "Don't take any chances. It's going to be dark soon. Be safe, Katie."

Katie swallowed hard. She knew how much yesterday's confrontation between them was weighing on Leblanc. But they were both professionals. They had put that behind them, and now would do what was necessary.

"Okay," Katie said. "I'll see you soon."

"I'll see you soon," he repeated.

Katie watched him jump out and hurry across the pier.

She knew how risky it could be, hunting down a suspect who was desperate, might be armed with a lethal weapon, and who was holed up in territory which he knew well. Leblanc was courageous and could hold his own in physical combat. He was not going to let her down, she was sure of it.

As she watched him splash his way to the waiting motorboat, she hoped with all her heart that he would be all right, because she didn't want to think too hard about what might play out there in the next few hours.

But the truth was that they were both heading into danger. The closer they got to the killer, the greater the chances were that one or the other of them would be involved in a violent showdown.

CHAPTER ELEVEN

Leblanc felt the boat surging through the strong waves as the island drew closer. Rain was soaking his face, cold and stinging.

Despite the dark and stormy weather, he felt determined to do his best. He needed to atone for his idiocy yesterday. Not just yesterday, he reminded himself. The seeds of this bad decision were sown long before, and had been ripening to a poisonous harvest.

Now he felt as if he'd had a second chance. As if, finally, he'd been able to look inside himself and see the wrong turns he had taken. Now, he had to succeed. He had to show that he could do this.

The motorboat began to slow down as it approached the island's steep, rocky beach. Once it stopped, Leblanc jumped off and splashed through the water to where two other officers were waiting for him.

A few boats were already on site. Police radios were crackling, the background noise at once familiar and disturbing in this isolated space.

"We're at a disadvantage here with the light, I'm afraid," the lead officer told Leblanc, handing him a flashlight. "We were about to call the search off when three people from the party saw the suspect flee. We have since got into position, checking the perimeter in case there is any sign of a boat he could use. So far we've seen nothing, but there are a lot of hiding places around the coast we haven't looked. However, we thought that a bigger priority was to work inward and try to bracket him. We've already sent home the civilians on the party. With this level of risk, we want police only going in. That means less of us, unfortunately, but there's a limit to the resources we have."

"Good idea," Leblanc said. "Do you know what he looks like?"

"The description was of a 'wild-looking' man. A short, scruffy beard, and wearing ragged clothing."

Leblanc knew that Sweeney could have grown a short beard since he'd been on the run. The timing allowed for it. But what could also not be ruled out was that this killer was not Sweeney and was, in fact, someone living wild on these islands who had now begun to commit a string of murders.

"I know you must have the search well organized," he said. "So I'll be happy to join in."

"We thought we'll start from this beach and fan out over the island. The woods in the middle where we think he fled are likely to be the most dangerous place, as there's a lot of cover and it's already getting dark. But he could be hiding anywhere."

Leblanc nodded, deciding to put himself forward for the riskiest part of the job.

"Can I be your eyes and ears in the thickest part of the woods?" he asked.

"Sure," the other detective agreed. "But watch out for yourself. Here's a radio you can use."

"Good luck," the other cop said, as his radio crackled with another burst of noise. "We're shifting now. Call in immediately if you see anything."

The lead officer checked his gun, and the others did the same.

"Get ready," he said.

Together, the small group headed into the woods

Leblanc took his position along the strung-out line of searchers, numbering about six.

As the party moved off, he walked straight into the trees, taking the route directly ahead that led to the thickest cover. He wanted to redeem himself. He wanted to help catch the killer—for Katie, for the task force, but also for himself.

The pebbles and rocks underfoot were compact and slippery, forcing him to tread carefully. The wind had dropped, but rain was still streaming down, and the trees were creaking and groaning.

Somewhere in the distance, he heard a scream. A seagull calling, he realized. Not more than that. And the crack that had just made him jump?

Was it a branch snapping?

Or the killer, creeping up on him?

He glanced around but all his flashlight illuminated was wet foliage and falling rain. He pressed on, moving from tree to tree, scanning ahead and around, his gun held ready. He was feeling afraid, but knew that was normal. Courage was not the absence of fear but rather, overcoming fear.

Every footstep made unavoidable noise, and in the distance, he could hear the muted sounds of the other searchers, but he tried to move as lightly as possible, trying to make less noise than the trees themselves.

The terrain, already difficult, became more so as it began to slope upward. Leblanc ducked under low branches and clambered over fallen trees. He moved as quietly as he could, not wanting to alert the suspect, and also not wanting to miss him completely in the deepening night.

He swung his flashlight around, searching. Shadows loomed in its beam.

The rain was finally easing off. A few drops still fell, and he could hear the occasional splash of water in the branches and feel the cool breath of the wind on his face, but the storm was beginning to move away.

He was making sure to keep a lookout for footprints, even though he knew the chances of finding any were unlikely, because the rain would have washed the prints away in the softer tracts of ground. But most of the terrain underfoot was stony, carpeted with leaves already brown and dead.

Leblanc looked around, listening intently. Something rustled nearby and his instincts flashed immediately to red alert. He stopped and turned to look, holding his breath, the beam of his flashlight pointed straight ahead.

He waited.

Nothing moved. He slowly began to breathe again. Then he listened.

What had that sound been?

He started moving forward again, pushing aside rough branches, stepping over leaves that crunched, his flashlight trained ever ahead in his search. He stopped again and listened.

Another branch rustled, but further in the distance this time, and he began to think that it was only an animal.

Even so, with a fugitive hiding, it was important to take every sound seriously. A man trying to hide could make the same small, rustling noises as an animal innocently going about its business.

What he now needed to ascertain was whether the sound was moving away from him, or toward him. If it was moving toward him, he might end up being a target.

He waited, unmoving. His spine prickled. He sensed that he was not alone in this dark knot of forest. So perhaps he needed to take the initiative now and flush the other man out. The element of surprise would be critical.

"Who's there?" Leblanc called sharply, shining his flashlight toward where he thought the sound had come from.

But then, suddenly, he sensed something rushing toward his head.

Instinctively ducking, flinging himself down, Leblanc narrowly avoided the rock that had been hurled in his direction. Jagged and large, it would have injured him severely had it found its target. The rock flew overhead and smashed into the bushes behind him.

Then, with a flurry of movement, he saw a man burst out from the trees ahead and run. A tall, rangy shape in the flashlight beam, he plowed headlong through the woods, ducking and diving around the branches as if he knew his way well through these woods.

"I have him! He's here!" Leblanc shouted, hearing cries of consternation from the team around him. "He's broken through the line!"

They might lose him if he went to ground somewhere in the thickets of the woods. But Leblanc realized he was plunging down the hill. That meant, worse still, he might have a boat hidden somewhere and be intending to flee the island and disappear out at sea in the night.

With no time to lose, Leblanc set off at a run, hoping that he could catch up with his would-be killer.

CHAPTER TWELVE

By the time Katie arrived at the house of the attempted carjacking victim, Will Abbott, it was nearly dark. On this gloomy, rainy day, she had to subdue a sense of panic that time had run away with them, and that nightfall would allow the killer to get a lead.

She parked outside the small house, a semi-detached home in Halifax with a neat, paved yard, and rang the bell.

Abbott opened up almost immediately.

He was a man who looked to be in his sixties. He was lean and fit looking, with tousled gray hair and stressed blue eyes, wearing a turtleneck sweater. She saw a graze on his face, and a dressing on the back of his hand.

"Will Abbott? I'm Agent Katie Winter from the task force," she introduced herself.

"Ma'am, I sure hope you can catch this guy. I can't believe such a thing happened. To me. Just a block from my home."

She saw his hands were shaking.

"Can you explain what happened?" Katie said, as he led the way inside and sat down in a small living room. She took the armchair opposite, even though she felt too impatient to want to sit. Rain pattered on the window glass.

"I was driving down to the harbor, and was stopped at a light when he ran up and smashed my window. It was like an explosion. The whole car shook. Before I could do anything, he'd reached inside, grabbed my wallet off the passenger seat, and the next thing he was hanging onto my wrist and literally dragged me out of the car."

"Were you badly hurt?" Katie looked again, in concern, at his visible injuries.

"No, I tried to fight him off, which was probably not the wisest decision, but I was panicking. Then the motorist behind me started honking on his horn. I think that made him have second thoughts about anything else he planned to do. I managed to get a kick in, and the guy behind jumped out of his car, and that's when he ran off and disappeared. There was only the one driver behind me, and he came to help me. He didn't chase after the criminal, which was probably just as well."

"Did you get a look at him?" she asked.

"Yes. He was a young guy. By that, I mean maybe in his twenties or thirties. He had short, dark hair and very angry-looking eyes. It was like he was frowning at me. He was very strong."

Katie felt her heart speed up. The description was a match for Sweeney. It was highly likely that this victim had been targeted by the escaped convict.

"Did you see which direction he went?" she asked.

"Yes." Moving to the living room window, he pointed. "You can see the road from here. He fled down that way."

"What's down that way?"

"It leads to the old dock area. It's not used anymore."

Katie thought about that.

"Did he come from that side also?" she asked.

"I'm not sure," the man said. "I only noticed him when he smashed my window."

"And have the police been here yet?"

"They have. One officer came around and helped me with the report, and he's just left. They said they were going to organize a search of the old dock area as soon as they could, but that it might take an hour or two to set up. They are short staffed because of the manhunt on the islands." He shook his head. "Now I'm wondering if they're looking in the wrong place. That dock area is due to be refurbished in a couple of months, they have big plans for it when spring comes and it'll soon be a very different place, but for now I must say it's not the first crime we've experienced where the criminal has fled there."

Katie considered his words. "I agree with you," she said.

She could be quicker than the police would be in searching this crime hotspot. It would be dangerous going in alone, but she had a gun and at this stage, it would be worth the risk. Time was critical.

"Thank you so much. I'm sorry this happened to you, but what you've said has been very helpful."

His stressed expression eased slightly. "I'm glad it has," he said.

Katie left, but she didn't even bother going to the car. Not when the criminal's bolt hole was so close by. She pulled up her jacket hood against the rain and jogged down the road that Will Abbott had pointed out.

She was holding out hope that on this rainy, cold evening he would have decided to hunker down in one of the disused buildings. One aspect that gave her a flare of hope was that she'd read that Sweeney was an arrogant, overconfident criminal. When he was committing his crimes he was reckless, and seemed to get on an adrenaline high that made him feel invulnerable. He'd done it in the past, and this carjacking, in daytime and in front of a witness, proved it again.

If that was true, it was all the more reason why he might think he wouldn't be found in this hiding place, and would plan to make a move after dark. That might be soon, so she needed to hurry.

Of course, that reckless mindset made him even more dangerous. For a moment, Katie wished she had Leblanc along with her. Right now, she missed and needed her partner, and had to gather her courage, knowing that there was no alternative with the shortage of manpower and that lives were at risk. She jogged on, approaching the disused docks.

The road led past some warehouses and a dilapidated shed, now derelict, before ending in a broken, fragmented parking lot in the old dock area.

She stopped, looking around.

This was a dark, dingy place, silent and abandoned.

As she stood there, a gust of wind blew up, pelting her with rain. She pulled her jacket collar closer around her and kept walking, stepping carefully across the rough ground, until she reached the beginning of the old dock.

There were a few old buildings on her right that she thought must once have been a central office. Then, to her left, she saw the high, dark shapes of warehouses.

Left or right? If she was a fugitive, where would she go?

Katie opted for left as the first choice. The space that a warehouse provided was the deciding factor. She walked toward the darkened doorway of the closest warehouse. There, she switched on her flashlight and paused, listening for any sounds of movement. She heard nothing.

Taking a deep breath, she moved through the partly open door.

The warehouse was huge, larger than she'd realized when she'd spotted it from outside. The roof was high, and crisscrossed with girders. The floor was covered in broken wood, and she had to tread carefully. It smelled of dust and oil, and more faintly of salt and brine.

Deeper inside the warehouse, there seemed to be a series of piled-up boxes. Was that movement near them?

Katie sensed it out of the corner of her eye and froze instantly, but it had been too quick and fleeting for her to make sense of it. It could have been a giant rat. But it could also have been a person, ducking out of sight.

She trod carefully over to the dust-covered boxes. The place felt dead and abandoned, but that didn't mean she was alone here. Adrenaline was pounding inside her as she walked forward. As she reached the boxes, a sudden gust of wind whipped through the warehouse, making her shiver.

Maybe she'd been mistaken about the movement. Or maybe it had just been the wind blowing a tarpaulin around. Katie felt another breath of cold air against her face. This place was drafty.

Crouching low, she moved sideways, examining the jumbled pile. She ran her flashlight over the heap, looking for any sign of a crouching figure beyond.

And then the wind gusted again and sent the box on top of the pile crashing down to the floor, splintering apart in a cloud of dust. Two others followed as the pile toppled and smashed.

The impact was thunderous in the still space. The sound echoed through the vast warehouse as dust billowed high in the air. Katie leaped back, her heart in her throat from the unexpected noise and movement.

She'd been startled by the bang. And someone else had, too.

From behind the boxes, a figure burst out, running at top speed for the far doorway. His footsteps slapped urgently on the dusty floor.

Katie caught a glimpse of short, dark hair and a powerful build, swathed in an old taupe jacket. It was him, she thought. Sweeney. She was sure of it. He'd been hiding out here and, startled by the bang, had broken and run.

And then there was no more time for thought, because she was pursuing him with all the speed she had.

CHAPTER THIRTEEN

"The man's here! He's running!" Leblanc shouted, hoping that the other cops in the island search party would be alerted in time to join the chase.

He was determined to keep pace with this man before he could reach a hiding place or jump into a hidden boat. He sprinted after him through the woods, his boots skidding over bark and leaves, wet branches whipping his face.

The man ran fast, with his head down, dodging around stunted bushes and rocks, and even jumping over a fallen tree.

Pounding across a wet patch of pebbles, Leblanc saw the man skid on the stones. He stumbled, half-fell, and scrambled up again.

That momentary slip had allowed Leblanc to gain a few valuable seconds. Striding as fast as he could, he was gaining on him, and felt determined that he might catch him.

But then he slipped on another tract of loose gravel. As he windmilled his arms to save himself, he stumbled over a tree root invisible in the gloom. Pain stabbed through his ankle and he gasped. He almost went sprawling, but put a hand down to save himself. Rough stones scoured his palm. There was no time to worry about these minor injuries. Time only to continue with the chase. The other man was gaining on him again. He ran with a loping, almost animal grace.

But Leblanc was determined that he would not escape, and that this man's police hunt would end here, now, tonight. Pursuing him furiously, he tried to put more effort into each stride, wincing from the pain in his ankle.

He blinked as a squall of rain surged, blowing into his eyes, but still he ran, following the crashing sound of the other man's footsteps through the woods.

Leblanc heard voices behind him now. The others had joined the chase. He was still in the lead, though, doing his best to gain the valuable yards that could make the difference between success and failure.

The fugitive was nearing the edge of the woods. And then Leblanc saw the man take a sharp left. He was heading toward a different part of the coast.

Fears about a hidden boat surged again. "He's going left!" he shouted, running as fast as he dared over the uneven terrain, his heart pounding in his chest.

Squalls of rain were blasting at him from the north. The storm had veered around, making everything difficult to see.

He could just make out the figure ahead of him, and Leblanc thought that the man was slowing down. Perhaps he was struggling to keep up the pace, starting to tire. That was a good sign. He would not be able to run much further.

Leblanc felt likewise. He was exhausted, his ankle was throbbing, but the hours in the gym in Sault Ste. Marie had earned him a level of fitness that he hoped would mean he'd be able to outlast him.

He was sure that this was the man who had committed these crimes. Running was a clear sign of guilt. This was his chance to arrest him, and put an end to the spree of murders that were traumatizing this community.

And he'd caught up enough to do it. He lunged toward the man, reaching out, grabbing him by the trailing hem of his ragged coat.

Leblanc was dragged forward by the force of his momentum. His feet left the ground. He felt himself falling, and then the ground was rushing toward his face.

No, he promised himself. He could not fail now. He could not lose. He clung on and felt the man stumble and fall, too, crashing to the ground. Leblanc gripped onto his coat desperately.

They rolled over on the stones and mud, grappling with each other. The man was stronger than he looked, and he was fighting Leblanc with the strength of total desperation.

Leblanc threw all his weight on top of him, pinning him down on the wet, muddy ground, but the man struggled and lashed out. In the dark, Leblanc barely saw the blow in time. He ducked, and it glanced off his shoulder.

He twisted the man's arm up behind his back, jerking it as hard as he could, trying to get purchase on the rough, slippery stones. Then he hissed in a breath as the man kicked back, catching him a lucky shot on the knee.

He sprawled down, and the man made a lunge for freedom. Grabbing onto him with even more resolve, Leblanc yelled again.

"Here! He's here!" while trying to avoid his stabbing elbows and thrashing feet.

And then, at last, backup arrived. To his massive relief, he heard the stamp of running footsteps, and two cops converged on the suspect, grabbing his flailing limbs.

They had done it. They had caught the man.

Now to find out who he was, what he was doing here, and what his involvement in the killings was.

Breathless and aching, Leblanc pushed himself up.

The rain had soaked him through, and the struggle on the ground had added to the damage. He was soaked to the skin, muddied, dirty, and torn. His hands were grazed, his knee felt bruised, and his ankle was throbbing.

But he felt a deep sense of satisfaction that despite the odds, he'd achieved his goal.

It had been so close. Looking through the gap in a rocky outcrop nearby, he could see the shape of a small motorboat, hidden from sight in a sheltered inlet.

Another minute and this fugitive would have been free and clear.

The man was helped to his feet by the cops who held his arms firmly. Wiping mud from his face, retrieving his flashlight which was shining in the bushes a few yards away, Leblanc got his first good look at him.

Immediately, with a thud of disappointment, he confirmed to himself what he'd already sensed in the struggle. This was not Sweeney. This man was wild-eyed, with a bushy beard and shoulder-length hair. He was wearing an old parka. Under the hair and beard, Leblanc guessed him to be in his forties.

However, he told himself that this merely confirmed Katie's tentative theory that the escaped convict and the island killer might be two separate people. Running was a sign of guilt.

How did he get down here? Why was he hiding out in the woods? Where was he based, and why had he fled?

"Your name?" Leblanc asked.

"I'm Denver. Miles Denver," the man muttered.

"Why are you on this island, Denver?"

"I—I'm just camping out here, man. I want to—to make a fresh start in life."

"On this island?" Leblanc asked incredulously.

"Yeah. I want to be alone here."

"Why did you run?"

"I heard you coming," he explained. "And I panicked. I didn't know what to do. I thought you were going to arrest me or something so I was running to hide in my tent."

"Why would we arrest you if you were innocent?" Leblanc asked.

"Because I don't think people are supposed to come and live on these islands. I know there are rules about fires and suchlike. It's a free world, man, but nobody can lay claim to the earth, and that's heresy."

His eyes flashed.

"How long have you been here?"

"A few weeks."

"A few weeks?" Leblanc echoed.

"Yes. About seven weeks."

"And you've been alone here?"

"A friend visited me a couple of times. Yesterday, and again earlier in the week. He comes over every so often. I go see him once in a while."

Leblanc sighed. "Okay. Do you have any ID? A wallet? Anything like that?"

"I… I don't have any ID on me. All I have is a wallet, but it's at my campsite. I live over there." He gestured a thumb over his shoulder.

"How far away is this campsite?"

"It's past this little headland," Denver explained. "There's a sandy beach there. You can see my tent from the beach."

"Let's go take a look at it."

He gestured to the cops to cuff the captive and then they set off, following Denver toward the rocky outcrop that overlooked the inlet.

The man was being cooperative, but Leblanc was still wary.

"Have you seen anyone else here on the island recently?" he asked him as they walked.

"No. I told you, a few people came, but I kept away from them."

"You were hiding a boat," Leblanc said. "What were you doing with it?"

"I—I was hiding it for a reason, man. Too many people are coming here, getting themselves drunk, stealing, breaking. I don't like that. I just fixed my boat. I don't want it stolen."

They walked down a steep pathway, between tall rocks, and then Leblanc suppressed a gasp of surprise as he shone the flashlight ahead and saw a small tent, set up in a sheltered grassy area surrounded by rocks.

The tent looked neat. There were even some plants growing nearby.

"Herbs, cabbages. I know how to farm," Denver said.

"Tell me about the friend who visited you yesterday." Now Leblanc needed to know if his movements could possibly be accounted for.

"He's an old work friend who lives on the peninsula. He sailed over yesterday morning and gave me a ride into town. My boat's motor was broken, so I was stranded here for a couple of weeks. Yesterday, I got paid and I could get the parts to fix it. I get disability, you see, because I lost part of my hand. I used to work at the sawmill out of town."

Having fingers missing might make it more difficult to wield the killing weapon, but Leblanc was more interested in the timeline. An alibi could clear him. Being stranded on the island would mean he'd been unable to kill the victims.

"What were your movements yesterday?"

"We bought the parts from the hardware store, Jackson's, in the morning. They know me in there. The manager, Tony, is a friend. I did some shopping, and we had food and a beer at the harbor in the afternoon. I paid. Then he sailed me back, and I spent most of today fixing up the motor. It's working now."

"What's your friend's name?"

"Herbert Christensen. I'll give you his number. We've been messaging back and forth for a few days, organizing this. I can show you the messages. He brought me some supplies a couple of days ago because I couldn't leave. He took a look at the boat and then sent me a list of what I should buy to fix it. I can show you. I just have to get my phone and turn it on. It's in the tent. I charge the power bank when I go into town, and charge the phone from there when I need it."

Leblanc sighed.

"Okay. Thank you," he said. He turned to the cops. "Can we confirm this?"

"I'll check out that entire timeline, and the messages," the closest cop said.

But, before the cops escorted Denver down the hill to the tent, Leblanc turned back to him.

"You need to be careful. This is not a good time to be living wild. There's a killer on the loose, and he's targeting uninhabited islands. You might find yourself with company you don't want if you stay here, and in trouble all over again," he warned.

Thinking of trouble, he suddenly wondered how Katie had been doing. He hoped her lead had panned out better than his. He took out his phone to see if she'd messaged, and felt a stab of worry when he saw the screen was still blank.

Was she okay? he wondered, with a clench of his stomach.

CHAPTER FOURTEEN

This fleeing man was Sweeney. Katie was sure of it as she launched herself in pursuit. The glimpse she'd had as he turned to bolt had been enough to convince her.

The escaped convict had followed her prediction of his movements and done what she'd thought he would do. He'd holed up in the warehouse, believing that he'd be able to lurk there unseen. His bravado and arrogance had gotten the better of him.

A lot of violent criminals suffered from hubris. Sweeney had just proved he was one, Katie knew, as she sprinted after him, all her senses on full alert, her inner strength and determination spurring her on.

Skidding around the corner after him, she exited the warehouse and sprinted down the narrow, unevenly paved track. She propelled herself between two vast shipping containers, darting through the small space.

She could hear his footsteps pounding ahead on a zigzag path. He was heading for the next-door warehouse. This area was clearly familiar to him. He'd been hiding here before now. That put her at a disadvantage, Katie thought, nearly losing her footing as she slipped on a patch of oily water.

There were too many possible hiding places and exits in this dilapidated area. He could get away if she didn't reach him fast enough. And she was losing him. He was outpacing her.

Katie lost sight of him as he darted between stacks of heavy shelving. She slammed to a halt and changed direction, shining the flashlight ahead, running as fast as she could around the outside of the shelves, trying to cut him off.

But his lead was already too great. She could hear him ahead of her, his loud footsteps echoing. The sound was growing fainter.

He was taking her on a dark and dangerous path, threading his way past abandoned boxes and piles of steel fittings. She was going to have to take more risks if she was going to catch him. Her only chance was to get ahead. To anticipate him. To catch him before he had a chance to react.

But then a piece of piping slid away as her foot landed on it. She skidded and fell. The metal pipe clanged away. Katie sprawled to the ground, rolling, doing her best to protect herself from the impact with the slick, hard concrete.

He spun around, on the defensive, and looked at her as she scrambled to her feet. He was breathing hard. In the flashlight beam, she saw fear dissolve into incredulity in his glowering features.

"One cop?" he said in astonished tones. "Only you?"

Too late, Katie realized that he'd believed a whole team was after him, not just a lone female agent. She saw his eyes, cold, brutal, and intelligent, instantly process the information.

Then Katie saw him make a decision. The look in his face told her all she needed to know.

To her astonishment, as she scrambled shakily to her feet, he charged straight at her.

Seeing her on her own, this man had chosen to attack. She saw vicious intent in his eyes as he neared her. She was taken so far by surprise she didn't even have time to get her gun out.

He was big and he was fast and he was determined to stop her in her tracks.

He tackled her brutally, with all the skill and force of a seasoned street fighter, and they both fell. She dropped her flashlight, groping desperately for her gun. They landed in a heap of legs and arms and struggling bodies, Katie was trying to protect herself, and to find some purchase.

She was trying to get her gun out of its holster, but this man was clinging to her, his hands grabbing for her face, her throat. He could easily put out one of her eyes. He would do something like that. She twisted her face away, trying to keep her vulnerable areas out of reach as she fought him off with all she had. He hung on as she struggled, his whole body weight bearing down onto her.

"Are you the only one, bitch?" he growled. "Are you the only one?" he asked her again, crushing her throat in a bruising grip.

Katie was choking, but she couldn't let herself be beaten by him. She couldn't let him win.

If she was going to get out of this, she had to do whatever it took. She flung up her head, smashing it against his, then hit him as hard as she could with her fist. He recoiled, and she thrust her elbow up and into his face.

He gasped in pain, then made another desperate grab for her. This time, she was able to avoid his grasp. She got hold of the steel piping that was lying on the ground and swung it at him.

She caught him with it. The blow glanced off his head, knocking him back. Her eyes widened as he slumped down.

He'd been knocked out cold. She'd done it.

Gasping with relief, trembling all over from the effort and the adrenaline, Katie got the cuffs off her belt and clamped them onto his wrists and ankles. When she was sure he was no longer going to be a threat or a flight risk, she then grabbed up her flashlight again and took a good look at his face.

The confirmation was now one hundred percent. Undoubtedly this was Sweeney. The coarse tattoo from his recent ID photo was just visible, gray and blurry on his neck.

He was already starting to groan and writhe on the ground. Not so much knocked out as temporarily stunned, but it had given her enough time.

She looked down at him, feeling an overwhelming sense of relief. She'd done it. The hunt was over. She'd captured the killer. And she'd done it on her own.

She felt no triumph, only thankfulness.

Quickly, she took out her phone, glad that it had survived the struggle, although the screen was cracked. At least she could make the calls she needed to. The very first one was to Leblanc.

He grabbed it up on the first ring. Anxiety resonated in his voice.

"What's happening your side?"

"I caught him," she said. Her voice sounded breathless. She knew that pursuit had taken a lot out of her.

"You got him?" he repeated incredulously.

"The victim was able to point the way where he fled. He was hiding out in the abandoned warehouses. I reckoned he'd still be there, that he was too arrogant to believe he'd be caught."

"This is such great news," Leblanc said. "We have him! The same day we started the search?"

"It's amazing," she agreed. "It took teamwork. It really took the efforts of everyone who helped out, and I know there were a lot of them."

"Yes. The amount of support from such a small community has been incredible. Even here on the island where I've just been chasing one of the suspects. Brave people, going out to the islands and into the unknown. Police, volunteers, citizens."

"I'm going to call Callum now and ask him to transport this criminal to the nearest police department," Katie said. "Do you want to meet me there? We need to interrogate him. Both of us should do that job, and as soon as possible. Let's get a confession out of him and put this case to bed."

But as she stared into the convict's dark, narrowed eyes, Katie had an uneasy feeling that he was going to resist every step of the way.

It would take all their combined skill and experience to crack the truth out of this man's hardened shell.

CHAPTER FIFTEEN

The bar was one of the most popular in Halifax, a noisy, crowded place. Rock music pumped. The place was packed with tourists, enjoying their vacation.

Sitting at the bar, grinning expansively, Garrison looked around, raising his glass in a toast with the three tourists he'd just met.

He was on vacation, too. Well, as of an hour ago. He'd knocked off work for the day, and this bar, in particular, was his favorite hangout.

Garrison wasn't his real name. It was the name everyone knew him by.

It was a good name. An easy, honest name. He'd chosen it because it was also the name of one of the biggest breweries in the wider area, the one that made the beers he enjoyed drinking the most.

That way, he could always say that Garrison was actually a nickname, if anyone asked. It would make a funny story, that he'd been given the name of his favorite beer by a friend, long ago. People would laugh at that story. He knew how to entertain.

He caught a glimpse of himself in the mirror. He looked genial, his dark, wavy hair roughly styled but neatly cut, the hint of tan from the wind and sun on his strong jaw that identified him as an outdoorsman.

He grinned at the thought of how much the island lifestyle agreed with him. The freedom, the space. The fact that his work was well-paying and easy.

And the after-work opportunities. Those were the cherries on the cake. The jam on the bread. His secret reward for the honest efforts of the day.

"Cheers," he said, still grinning at himself, but now turning to the three female tourists he was in conversation with. "It's a fine evening to be having a celebration."

He lifted his glass again, feeling happy and confident. The three women nodded, with large smiles.

They liked him, and they were happy. He felt warm inside. It was good to be in a place like this. He was glad he was able to come here and socialize. He enjoyed tourists. Everything about them. He really, really did. They brought opportunity in so many ways.

These lovely ladies were sharing a bottle of champagne.

"It's a great evening for it," the closest woman said. She was a pretty, slender brunette with a smile that seemed to go on forever. "We've so enjoyed our time here."

"And when you're not on vacation, tell me what you do," Garrison said.

"I'm an artist," the brunette replied, looking pleased that he'd asked. "A sculptor. I do my best work when I'm in the wild, so I like to spend as much time in nature as possible."

"How amazing! You know, I always have the utmost admiration for creatives. To make a living from that, you must be really talented."

"I've got a good reputation," she said, blushing at the praise. "And I'm lucky that my pieces sell well."

"And what's your name?" he asked, turning to the second woman. She was older, her blonde hair showing some streaks of gray. She, too, was attractive and looked like she had a good sense of humor.

"My name's Samantha," the woman said. "I'm a teacher. I was telling my friends earlier, the best thing about teaching is that the vacations allow you to take time off when you need it. And you do need it."

"Do you work in a private school?" he asked her.

They were all laughing, drinking champagne fast, and he thought they were feeling a little giddy.

"Yes, my school went on vacation the day before we arrived. I cleared my desk and made a break for it."

Garrison looked at her more closely, letting his eyes do the smiling. For a moment he visualized her alone on the boat. He wondered what question he would ask her, and what her reply would be.

That was the key. The reply was always key. It was what allowed him to make the decision about what would happen next.

She smiled back at him, holding his gaze and flirting a little. She clearly wanted to impress him. How sweet.

"What are your favorite subjects to teach, Samantha?" he asked.

"I'm an English and history teacher," she said. "I enjoy teaching students about ancient civilizations and mythology. I find they're extremely interested in that if you teach it well. I also teach modern history, of course. And surprisingly, I find a lot of my students love poetry."

"Poetry is most definitely something that feeds the soul," he agreed. "And what about you?" He turned to the third woman, round faced and rosy cheeked.

"I'm a chef," the third woman said. She had a brisk manner and an air of competence about her.

"That's a difficult job. Long hours. People think it's glamorous."

"Oh, they so do!" She laughed, nodding agreement.

"You must have a lot of stamina."

"I have that in spades," she said.

"And what do you cook?" he asked.

She smiled.

"I work for an Italian restaurant, so I can literally make any Italian dish in my sleep. But I love experimenting with my own recipes. I love to find new flavors and new ways of combining flavors to make something entirely new. There's nothing more exciting than cooking something you've never cooked before."

"I can see you're an adventurous chef. I'd love to eat at your restaurant someday," he praised.

They were all smiling. He'd made them feel good, he knew. He'd made them feel happy and interesting.

Garrison was lucky. He had a natural charisma. He could make people feel special, and along with that came the ability that if he suggested something, they would go along with it.

He was a lucky man. He knew it.

Of course, there was the most important question of all, one that he always asked when the time was right.

The question depended on who he had with him. But he always gave that choice. Always. People needed to choose.

He smiled as he thought about some of the answers, and what had followed. Those scenes were set in a very different place from this brightly lit bar where music thumped.

The screams that followed the wrong answer were like music to him, though.

But even as he focused on the trio, his gaze roamed the room. These women wouldn't work for him. He wouldn't be able to get one alone, and more importantly, he'd discovered they were heading home tomorrow. That was the celebration. Their last night on the island.

He tipped his beer back, enjoying the flavor of hops on his tongue.

He grinned at the man sitting opposite him at the large, half-circle bar. That man was clearly on vacation. He seemed to be with his father, who looked in his sixties. Garrison would bet a lot of money they were here to fish.

Gazing at them, he wondered if they were going to be together for the entire vacation. Or whether there would be an opportunity to get one of the two to go out separately. He didn't mind which one.

His mouth was wide and smiling but as he stared at them, his gaze was cold and calculating.

The inner being that he kept hidden most of the time flared into evil life, sending a thrill of excitement through him as he thought of doing what he needed to, again.

It might be worth going over to the men and bidding these lovely ladies goodbye, he thought. His beer was finished. It was as good a reason as any to leave this particular party.

As he was about to make his move, his gaze was caught by a woman in the corner of the bar.

She was standing at the edge of the room, as if she was unsure about entering. There was an air of quiet reserve about her, but he didn't think it was due to a lack of confidence.

She was tall and slender, with thick, pale blond hair and deep blue eyes. She was most definitely a tourist. The sheaf of maps in her hand clued him to that.

And she was alone.

He turned back to his group.

"Ladies, it's been lovely meeting you. If you'll excuse me, I'm going to get myself another beer and then do the rounds. That's the thing about being a local. I can see a lot of friends here who'll be expecting me to stop by and say hi."

"It's been lovely meeting you, Garrison," they chorused enthusiastically.

Giving them his best smile, Garrison stood up.

They would never know how lucky they'd been. How he would have loved to let his real self loose on them, one by one, to get them out into the wilds, to see the terror on their faces as they realized who he was and the hunt began.

But there was a thrill in their not knowing, too. It made it even more fun that some didn't know his hidden side.

Garrison stood up and ambled over to the bar, glancing in the direction of the blonde and giving her a quick, friendly grin.

There was no hurry to make his way to her. The best things in life were worth the wait.

CHAPTER SIXTEEN

Katie sensed an atmosphere of excitement and triumph in the police department as soon as she walked in. Jovial voices and laughter were coming from a nearby office. Someone was on the phone in the corner of the lobby, and she heard the words "arrested by the agent."

Callum was waiting at the front desk, looking satisfied.

"A job extremely well done, Agent Winter," he said. "That was one of the most effective takedowns I've heard about, and single-handed, too. Sweeney was violent and dangerous, and that took courage as well as skill."

"It was touch and go at one stage," Katie admitted, rubbing her shoulder, which still ached from the fall.

At that moment, Leblanc rushed through. He was carrying two brimming cups of coffee. Never had Katie seen such a welcome sight.

"Katie." His face lit up to see her and she felt a surge of warmth inside her, too.

"Thanks for the coffee," she said, feeling grateful as he pressed one of the steaming cups into her hand.

"You caught him. On your own. That deserves more than coffee," he said.

Katie held her steaming cup between her hands, sipping at the scalding, sweet liquid, drinking in the taste of it. Right now, coffee hit the spot better than anything else she could think of.

"It was a group effort. And everyone involved deserves the praise," she said.

"We're busy setting up what you need in the interview room," Callum told her. "We have the suspect securely held. I'm going to go through and make sure it's prepared for the interrogation."

He headed down the corridor, and Katie turned to Leblanc, curious about what he'd had to handle out there on the island. He was still drenched, scratched, and decidedly muddy, although obviously on too much of an adrenaline high to worry about his condition.

He looked somehow vindicated and at peace with himself, but she had no idea whether this was because he'd withstood danger out there on the island, or because he'd made the decision that this was his last case. Anxiety flared inside her at these thoughts.

"What did you have to deal with?" she asked.

Leblanc shook his head. "Our suspect was a man who'd decided to live wild. He'd set up a tent on the island, but hadn't been anywhere for a couple of weeks as his boat's motor broke. Yesterday, a friend took him to the peninsula to buy what he needed to fix it. The local cops confirmed all his movements and checked the messages proving the timeline. He's cleared. I felt sorry for him, in a way."

"So, just in the wrong place at the wrong time," Katie agreed.

Leblanc seemed committed to the case, she thought with relief.

"Exactly. So, how did your takedown play out?" he asked.

"I had to chase Sweeney all the way through an old warehouse. And do you know, the only reason I got him was that he turned around and saw I was on my own, and decided to attack me? He clearly thought a woman would be easy pickings for him. If he'd run, he would have gotten away. Hubris." Katie shook her head.

"For sure," Leblanc agreed.

Katie drained her coffee and he did the same.

At that moment, Callum hurried back. "He's all yours. Ready and waiting." He led the way along the corridor, toward the interview rooms.

Katie felt keyed up and ready to go as she and Leblanc entered the small, brightly lit room and sat opposite the convict.

The overhead fluorescent light was harsh, and the neat, bright white space had a very no-nonsense, intimidating atmosphere.

The problem was, Katie immediately saw, that Sweeney didn't look intimidated.

He was glowering at them from under those thickset brows with a defiant expression on his face. Katie tried to ignore his hostility. This was never going to be an easy interrogation. It was lucky that the evidence itself was already so compelling. The timeline, the related crimes, then the spike of killings as this convicted murderer had arrived on the peninsula.

But even so, logistics and details were important to wrap the case up tight. Katie was determined to do everything she could to make sure that happened, and that Sweeney was convicted of all the murders he'd committed.

She put her files on the table and opened the folder, taking out her pen and notebook.

"We're going to be asking you questions relating to your movements and activities here in the past few days," she said sternly.

"But I don't have to answer, right?" Sweeney scowled. His voice was deep and throaty. "I have a right to remain silent."

"You have a right to do that, of course," she said. "But the sooner you can tell us what happened, the sooner we can close this."

"How's that going to help me?" Sweeney said.

Leblanc half-rose, leaning threateningly over the other man.

"You know what you've done. You might as well go for a guilty plea. You won't get reduced jail time but that's not the only thing you need to think about right now."

"What do I need to think about?"

Leblanc stared him down angrily. Katie could see he had no time for this defiant, brutal killer. She wondered if, deep down, he was reminded of Hugo Gagnon. This man was as entitled and unrepentant as she imagined Gagnon must have been. She was sure Leblanc was triggered by his attitude.

"You need to think about your treatment and privileges. If you cooperate now, you'll have an easier time inside. Trust me, there are levels of treatment, and you don't want to be at rock bottom. Especially since there's clearly a reason why you broke out. Didn't like it much inside? How about imagining it gets worse? If you're capable of doing such a thing. If not, you'll find out the hard way."

"So I'll cooperate," Sweeney said in surly tones. "I got out of jail. I was trying to survive. I stole some stuff. I didn't deserve to be caught."

"You're leaving out a lot of details," Katie said in a firm, steady voice.

"I don't have to tell you anything more," Sweeney threatened.

"Ultimately, the evidence will speak," Katie said. "You have the choice to confirm it now. Not too much choice, but neither did your victims."

Sweeney's jaw set. "You guys are trying to set me up here. I can see you are."

"How did you travel out to the islands?" Leblanc pushed.

"Islands? What islands?"

Leblanc leaned closer again. "Don't play games."

"I'm not playing games," Sweeney snapped. "You're the one doing that."

"The islands where you killed your victims. We know you were there. We need to know how you transported them there, and what you said to them. What boat did you use? Where is it? Where's the weapon?"

Sweeney shrugged. "I guess it's up to you to find that out, isn't it?" He gazed at them slyly. "Do you have evidence? Maybe not. If you're pushing me to confess, then I'm guessing you don't."

Katie shook her head. "You're not fooling anyone, Sweeney. We know you got out by boat."

"Who says I did? Prove it."

"Let's go back to the beginning," Katie said. "When did you arrive on the island?"

"I'm not answering any more questions. I've said all I'm going to say." He looked furious.

Katie's head was beginning to ache. She had a strong feeling Sweeney wasn't going to budge. He'd sensed they didn't know the details and was going to be as evasive as he could. They were only putting themselves in a weak position by pressuring him now.

And it had been a long day. On top of everything they'd had to deal with, a prolonged questioning was not going to get a miracle result.

She hoped that if she could sow the seeds of doubt in his mind, they might interview a different Sweeney tomorrow.

"It's up to you," Katie said. "This is going to be the first night of the rest of your life in jail. Remember that what you say now will influence the outcome of your sentencing and treatment. It could make a difference in which prison you get assigned to. Don't think we can't influence that. We can and will. You've got the rest of your life ahead of you to live, whatever happens. I hope you'll think on it."

She held his gaze and he looked away first. That was something, at least. Then she stood up from the chair and walked out, together with Leblanc.

It was time to call it a night. They needed to get food, get warm, and get some rest to refuel and regroup for another round of interrogation in the morning.

Katie fervently hoped that by tomorrow, her words would have an effect. They needed to fill in the gaps and details which would provide substance to the case.

For the time being, they had the killer firmly behind bars. The search could be called off. The teams could get some well-earned rest. And everyone could sleep easy knowing that no more murders would occur.

At least, so Katie hoped.

She was experienced enough to know that without a confession, there was always going to be an unwelcome sliver of doubt in that regard.

CHAPTER SEVENTEEN

Heidi Nielsen smiled at the man opposite her as the sea breeze ruffled her blond hair. She'd had too many glasses of wine back there in the bar. It had been warm and cozy.

And the inevitable had happened. A man had invited her for drinks at his place.

The man was good-looking—tall, dark-haired, with a short beard. He was a local guy who lived on a smaller island nearby. He'd told her all of this over the four drinks they'd shared.

Now, his place was where they were headed, out on the sea, and she felt filled with a sense of adventure. This was what vacation was all about.

Meeting interesting people always enthused her, and this guy sure was interesting. Even his name was unusual. Garrison. He had so many experiences and stories. He was very entertaining.

He was very handsome. He was well dressed, and he had such a presence. On top of all that, he was full of fascinating stories. She'd learned so much in such a short time. Like how he had been a soldier in the war. She wasn't sure which war exactly, but somewhere in the Middle East.

"I know it's not the most glamorous of jobs," Garrison said. "Hard, dangerous work most times. But it was the one I had. I did my duty."

Briefly, Heidi felt a flash of guilt for her husband, who'd paid for this vacation and then been laid up with a bad bout of stomach flu before their departure. He was planning to join her later, when he was well, but in the meantime, she was enjoying the time on her own. She knew she should not, strictly speaking, be going to do what she was thinking about.

But then again, she'd had four glasses of wine. And she was in a foreign country. She was entitled to experience all the local customs and feel a little wild.

At least, out on a boat sailing to another island, whatever happened, her husband would not know what she was getting up to.

Garrison said he was a boat captain who traveled a lot from harbor to harbor. That meant he would be gone tomorrow, she knew. A quick fling before he left would be something to put to one side as a fond memory.

"Perhaps you're a little cold? Do you want a jacket?"

He moved closer, putting his arm around her as if to protect her from the chilly breeze.

He'd been flirting with her in the bar. And now, she sensed the flirting was at a new level. Everything was so easy on vacation. She hadn't even bothered to remove her wedding ring. He could take her as he found her.

And Heidi didn't want to submit to the conventions of marriage while she was alone—she wanted a little fun. Somewhere, her mother would probably be shaking her head in disapproval. But she was not her mother.

"This is a beautiful part of the world," he told her. "These islands are incredibly scenic. This one we are coming up to now, where my cottage is, is my favorite."

"Really? Why?" she asked. "What's so special about it?"

The boat engine was loud. Garrison had to lean in close to her to be heard.

"I love the nature here. It's more than just physical beauty. It has a special feeling about it. I can't quite describe it. It's just a feeling I get when I'm here. A feeling that I am at one with the elements."

Heidi nodded. She could see what he meant.

Garrison maneuvered the boat expertly alongside the rocky shore, then hopped out onto the beach.

"Come on," he said, holding out his hand. "I'll help you off."

Heidi joined him and waded through the shallow sea to the shore, squealing as the icy water lapped her ankles. Garrison held out his hand and helped her up onto the small beach. He turned back and picked something up from the boat. In the dark, she couldn't see what it was but thought it was a walking stick. Right now, there was just enough moonlight to see the dim landscape ahead, but she guessed in the woods it would be darker.

"Nice island," Heidi said. "Lovely and private."

Garrison grinned. "Wait till you see my cottage. It's a great spot for what I have in mind."

Heidi was sure he knew what they both had in mind.

"I need to ask you a question," he said, and his voice sounded suddenly serious.

"What's that?" she asked, looking up at him, but his face was difficult to see in the dark.

"The way I think, when I meet someone like you, is this. You can do what you know you should do, or you can do what you feel like doing. Which do you choose?"

Heidi felt like this was a big, important question.

"I think I will do what I feel like doing," she said softly.

"And I will do the same," he agreed with a smile in his voice.

She stared at him. In the dim moonlight, his face was unreadable. Had there been something strange in his tone?

"Come on," he said, holding out his hand.

He led her up through the rocky beach and onto the path that wound through a dense copse of trees.

The track was barely visible, but Garrison led the way confidently.

Even so, Heidi was suddenly starting to have doubts.

A cottage? On this island? Was it real? She didn't think this track looked well enough used for Garrison to tread along it every day.

"How far do we have to go?" Heidi asked, trying to make it sound like a light chat, and not show that she was getting worried.

Garrison stopped and turned to her. She saw the flash of white teeth in his shadowy face.

"I told you, you will have to wait till you see it." He leaned in and whispered, "You like it that we're alone together, don't you?"

Heidi felt her panic growing. He was leading her further away from the shore. She wasn't sure she even knew how to get back.

They were inside a dense copse of trees, and she could not see what lay beyond. She felt thoroughly disoriented in the gloom, and was beginning to realize what a terrible idea this had been.

He had been so charming, so witty, so cute. Somehow, she'd forgotten that she was alone with a stranger, in a place she didn't know at all, and that nobody knew where she was. She'd forgotten all her fears—because she'd been distracted by their conversation and the way he'd paid her attention.

She'd been so focused on what might be about to happen. Now, that seemed like folly. How had she gotten onto a deserted island with a man she had met only a couple of hours ago? She knew nothing about him. And she was beginning to doubt the existence of this fictitious cottage.

"I want to go back," she said.

"You do? But why?" His voice was hard now. There was a different tone to it.

"This has been a mistake." She could hear the shrillness in her own voice. "I made a mistake coming out here."

"That wasn't your mistake. Your mistake was answering the question wrong."

Now there was not just menace in his voice, but raw threat.

At that moment, she took a good look at what was in his right hand.

It was not a walking stick. How drunk, how trusting had she been to think that? It was a long, wicked-looking steel spear with an ugly blade. Terror, icy and implacable, washed over her as she saw it.

Heidi screamed. She turned and ran, crashing her way along the path, stumbling over the undergrowth, twigs and leaves whipping her arms. She'd been a fool. So stupid.

Behind her, she heard his laugh, that jolly belly laugh she'd enjoyed so much in the bar. Then she heard his footsteps pounding behind her, fast and sure.

Then something hit her, a massive blow in the back, and she knew nothing more.

CHAPTER EIGHTEEN

The next morning, at seven-thirty a.m., Katie climbed out of the car and walked up to the RCMP police department, with Leblanc close behind her. She felt refreshed and invigorated after a good night's sleep that she'd never expected to have. She was ready to continue with the interrogation. Even though Sweeney was denying all the way down the line, she felt confident of breaking through his defenses this morning. Especially after a big cup of coffee and an excellent hotel breakfast.

Leblanc, too, looked clear eyed, and cut a stylish figure in his fresh, clean clothes. He was almost unrecognizable this morning, with his well-brushed hair, compared to the muddied, grimy man who'd fought in the wilds of the island last night.

It was a cool, bright morning. The sky was clear. A cold sun was blazing. The wind coming off the sea was brisk, and she found it invigorating.

The lack of clouds made it easier to see the rugged beauty of their surroundings, she thought, taking a look around her at the mountains on the horizon, and the coastline a few hundred yards away in the other direction, before walking in.

"Morning, Katie," Callum greeted her.

"Morning," she said.

Now that she was inside the musty warmth of the police department, she felt the seriousness of her job descend again. The time for relief and celebration and admiring the promise of the sunny day was over. Now, Katie was firmly focused on getting what she needed from the arrested criminal who had spent the night under police guard, and who was now awaiting the second round of questioning before the charges against him were officially completed.

"Are we going to use the same tactics today?" Katie murmured to Leblanc. "Or should we go in separately?"

Leblanc frowned. "We need to change things up. Let's go in one by one."

"I agree. Do you want to take the first round?"

"I'll do that," Leblanc said. Before he headed into the room, he hesitated.

"Katie, I wanted to tell you again how sorry I am. For everything that happened in the past few days. For my decisions. They were wrong."

Katie felt surprised. It must have taken a lot for Leblanc to say those words. She knew how proud—okay, to be truthful, how stubborn—he was.

And she was glad he'd put this topic on the table, because it had been eating away at her insides and causing her a flare of worry whenever she thought about it.

"I want to be able to trust you. And for you to trust me," she said slowly.

A silence fell between them. She could tell he was struggling with what he wanted to say next, and she was patient.

"I know," he said finally. "And I know I let you down."

"I don't want you to make decisions because you're worried about letting me down. I would rather you made them after being honest with yourself," she pointed out.

"You're right." He looked her in the eye. "And I'm trying to be honest now. With myself, and with you. I am sorry. I'm sorry for how I manipulated things. I'm sorry that I got sidetracked by this idea of revenge and didn't tell you. I let my own emotions get in the way. I messed up the trust between us, badly. It would have gotten worse if you hadn't intervened."

He drew a deep breath. "And I understand if you don't want me as your partner in the future."

"The main thing to do now," Katie said, "is to learn from this. If we can't trust each other, we're finished. We should be able to make decisions based on what's right, and not on what we think the other person wants to hear. Because we can only work together if we're honest with each other."

Leblanc nodded. "That's a hard lesson."

"But an important one," Katie added.

"Thank you, Katie," he said. Then he hesitated. "Do you think you can ever forgive me?"

She thought about it. She didn't ever want to feel the way she'd felt again, turning away from his apartment door, utterly shocked by the vengeful intent behind his decision to take the Paris job. She'd felt as if he'd taken a knife and stabbed her in the back with it. She'd felt lost.

But on the other hand, he'd told her he'd rethought, and regretted his choices. And this was her partner. If they couldn't trust each other, they were sunk.

Also, everyone made mistakes. When faced with the level of pain and loss he'd experienced, which she understood only too well, it was not unforgivable to have strayed down the wrong path.

"I think I can," she said, and saw him nod in relief. Then he gave her a tentative smile. "Now let's get to work and put Sweeney away for life, okay?"

"I'm game," Katie agreed.

She watched through the glass as Leblanc walked into the interview room. Sweeney glanced up as soon as he saw him. His hands were cuffed in front of him, and he looked cold and sullen.

"I didn't expect to see you again," he muttered. "The way you bailed on the last interrogation, I thought you'd decided I was no longer worth your time."

"I'm here because I owe it to the victims," Leblanc said. "And because I'm taking my job seriously."

Katie held her breath. It was subtle, but Leblanc's voice had changed. There was a quiet, controlled power behind it.

"Taking your job seriously?" Sweeney sneered. "I don't think so. You're looking for a shortcut. A scapegoat."

Keeping his temper, Leblanc replied, "Tell me your movements after you broke out of jail. Where did you go?"

"I got some supplies. Got some cash. I hid away in the back of a truck going across the border. I got lucky and nobody checked it," Sweeney said carelessly.

"And how did you manage to keep away from the police for so long?" Leblanc asked.

Sweeney shrugged. "I'm a smart man. I laid low until the coast was clear."

"When did you arrive here in Halifax?"

"A few days ago."

At least he was getting answers, Katie thought, feeling more positive that they might obtain the truth.

"Where did you get the boat? What boat did you use?"

Sweeney stared at him. "What boat are you talking about?"

Katie sighed. Just as Leblanc was getting to the core of the questioning, Sweeney was derailing the angle.

"The boat you used to go to the island," Leblanc said, his voice calm and even. "The one you used to kidnap your victims."

"You must be thinking of someone else," Sweeney said defiantly. "What, are you short on suspects that you're trying to pin everything on me? I'm innocent, man."

"We both know that's not true," Leblanc said.

Katie felt frustration flare inside her. This was not going to be easy. They could well be here the whole day if Sweeney persisted in talking in circles. He, after all, had all the time in the world. They were the ones under pressure to wrap up the case and press charges that were as solid as they could be.

He was a seasoned criminal and knew the ropes. He knew their weak points. He was smart and would look to capitalize instantly on any opportunity he sensed.

This was not going to be easy.

"Okay, look, let's go back to the islands for a minute," Leblanc said. "You're telling me you didn't go to any of them?"

Sweeney shook his head angrily. "Who do you think you're talking to? Some other guy? Who put you up to this?"

At that moment, Katie's phone, which was on silent, began buzzing in her pocket. She stepped outside the observation room to take the call, seeing that it was Scott on the line.

She guessed her boss was calling to congratulate them but wished that they had made better progress with the interrogation. She'd feel she deserved the praise more.

"Morning, Scott," she said.

"Katie. The suspect, Sweeney. He's still in custody?"

"Yes," she said, surprised. "We're questioning him now. Why?"

She felt a chill. She didn't like the tone of his voice. Stress was thrumming from his words.

"There's been another murder. This morning, a sailboat crew saw a woman's body on a beach. She's been identified as Swedish tourist Heidi Nielsen. I made a call immediately, and the hotel confirmed that they called a cab for her at five p.m. yesterday afternoon to go into town."

"What?" Katie said. She couldn't believe it. That was simply impossible. At five p.m., she'd been speaking to the carjacking victim. At five p.m., Sweeney had been hiding out where he'd fled.

There was no way he could have been picking out another victim at that time. Defeat crashed down on her.

They had their convict, but he was not the perpetrator of these crimes. Just as she'd feared inwardly, there was a reason they were getting nowhere with their questioning.

The killer was someone different, and they now needed to move at double the speed to track him down.

CHAPTER NINETEEN

Staring down at the slumped figure on the rocky shore, Katie felt a sense of utter disbelief. Beside her, she heard Leblanc swear softly under his breath.

This killer was growing bolder. He was not even bothering to kill in the deep wilds of the islands anymore, in places where bodies might remain hidden until they were consumed by the small predators, leaving nothing more than bones.

This was like a challenge to the police. Audacious, arrogant, and brutal.

The crime scene tape flapped softly in the breeze. The sunlight threw the rocks and shadows of the trees into harsh relief.

The seagulls wheeled overhead, screeching.

"It's lucky she was found so early," Callum said. He was bustling around and managing the scene. "The fishing boats don't usually sail this way at low tide, but a small boat took this route through the islands by chance."

"Did they disembark when they saw her?" Katie asked.

"No. They saw the body and immediately called it in. It was two local fishermen who'd participated in the search and were aware of the need to preserve the scene."

"That's good, at least," Katie said. "Perhaps there will be something to find. Something leading us back to him."

Feeling heavy hearted, she moved forward to stare down at the latest victim.

"It's the same killer. Without a doubt," Leblanc confirmed in a quiet voice.

The giant crimson stain on the back of the blond woman's cream-colored coat confirmed it.

It could be a copycat crime, Katie knew, but she didn't think so. It was far more likely that Sweeney had in fact been giving them accurate information. He'd admitted—sort of—to other crimes but they'd struck a blank wall when questioning him about the islands and the murders. He'd gotten angry and defensive and started complaining he was being framed.

And now, his reaction made sense, she thought.

Katie stepped back. The forensic team was already busy at work and she wanted to give them the space they needed to move as fast as possible.

"We'll do an initial examination." The dark-haired coroner looked up at her. "Try to establish basic parameters, like the time of death. And then we'll take this body straight in for an urgent postmortem."

"I hope that will tell us more," Katie said, grateful that they were able to give this such priority. The postmortem results might be critical in terms of evidence with this recently murdered woman, although the end results were still a few hours away.

Unless… A thought occurred to Katie. Unless there might be more evidence on the island.

She walked further up the beach. What had happened? How had this victim ended up here on the rocky shore?

And what had occurred in the minutes before her death?

That was something that needed further investigation, she decided.

Treading carefully over the rocks toward the wooded area, she scrutinized the ground closely. Unpleasant as it was to try and get into this killer's head, Katie knew she had to. It was imperative to try and understand the mindset of the man she perceived now to be a violent, overconfident killer.

Somehow, he'd managed to lure or coerce this woman out to a remote island at night.

She thought back to the other crime scenes. Every victim had been struck from behind. Therefore, there must have been a moment, too late, where the victims realized they were in mortal danger and started running for their lives.

That was part of what compelled this killer to bring them to such a wild, uninhabited place. Getting into his mind, feeling slightly sick with horror, Katie realized that the chase must be the reason.

It was the sense of victory over the victims, relishing the moment that they knew they were his prey, which made him want to bring them here. He had to see them running for their lives, before dealing the killing blow.

The chase, the tracking down and the fleeing, must be the whole experience that he enjoyed.

Cruelty, she thought. Evil to a degree she could never understand. But she had to force herself to try and understand it. She was starting again, with a fresh slate. The preconceptions she'd had, believing that

Sweeney was the murderer, now had to be put aside. Everything she'd linked back to his history and mindset was no longer valid.

Now she had to start from scratch in building the ideas, the impression, of the individual this killer really was.

It was a tough, daunting job, all the more demoralizing that it was coming so soon after they thought they had their man.

But the one point in their favor was that this body had been spotted and called in, with the scene untouched.

So, was there anything on the island that could tell them how and why this had happened?

Had there been a chase, as she suspected? The dense wooded area seemed to her to be the best place to start.

She ducked under the crime scene tape and stepped over the rocks, heading toward the woods. Leblanc hurried over to walk beside her.

"You think they might have gone up here first? That he engineered some kind of a chase, and got her while heading back to the boat?" he asked.

Katie felt reassured that he was on exactly the same page as her and had been thinking through the killer's movements in the same way.

"Yes. I'm theorizing that he did that. I think it's how he gets his thrills."

"Unreal," Leblanc muttered as he trod carefully over the ground, peering at the pebbles and twigs and fallen leaves.

The sun's rays filtered through the branches, and she felt increasingly uneasy that they might find nothing in this unforgiving terrain. Telling herself not to give up too soon, Katie trod further, trying to keep a hopeful attitude and an open mind.

And then, she caught her breath as she stared down at a muddy section of track.

"Fresh footprints!" she said. "Quick, Leblanc, look here. She wasn't killed as soon as they arrived on the beach. She must have walked inland for a while, with the killer. And then he chased her. That must have given him a sick thrill. Seeing her run in terror the whole way back to the beach, where he caught up and murdered her, not even caring her body would be in full view."

In a moment he was beside her.

"Yes. You can see blurred tracks in both directions crossing this muddy patch. It looks as if her imprints coming back were deeper."

Katie nodded solemnly. Undoubtedly this woman had realized she was in danger and had been running for her life.

But what about the other prints? The bigger ones? Those were the ones they needed to focus on now, and she felt hope surge inside her as they stared down.

It was the first actual sign of the killer they'd had. It was little more than a couple of sole prints in the mud, but it was something they could use.

It would give shoe size. Shoe type. They had a new starting point. Something to fill the disturbing blankness.

"There are shoe prints here!" she called, hearing the excitement in her own voice.

"This way!" Callum, who was managing the scene, called to the forensic crew. "We need to tape off this area and measure the prints!"

This would hopefully not be the only information this fresh scene would yield. Perhaps, with this new victim being so recently discovered, there might be more information on the weapon that this psychopath had used.

Until then, she knew their next step must be to try and track the victim's movements, and see if there was any clarity on where she went. That might give them an important clue.

"Let's take a drive to the hotel where Heidi Nielsen was booked in," she told Leblanc.

CHAPTER TWENTY

The hotel where Heidi Nielsen had stayed was an attractive building, with a dark wood frontage and well-tended grass and plants outside. When Katie climbed out of their loaned RCMP vehicle with Leblanc, she was surprised by how far out of town it was. This was a few miles away from Halifax itself, on a remote part of the coast.

The manager was waiting anxiously at the hotel's main entrance, clearly on the lookout for them after Katie had called twenty minutes earlier.

The pretty, dark-haired woman looked upset and stressed.

"We're from the task force," Katie said, hurrying over to her.

"I literally can't believe this has happened. One of our guests? And it must have happened just after the search was called off? I thought they said the killer had been found?"

Leblanc nodded grimly.

"We were hunting the escaped convict suspected of committing these crimes. We arrested him yesterday evening. Unfortunately, he's not the killer responsible for these island murders."

"He wasn't?" the woman asked, her eyes widening.

"No. His whereabouts were already accounted for when your guest was murdered."

"So, who is responsible?"

"We don't know the identity of that person yet. But we're doing everything possible to find him and capture him. This means we need to ask you some questions, to see if there's any information on Heidi Nielsen's movements."

"I'll do whatever I can to help," the woman said. She led the way inside.

The place smelled of polished wood and good coffee, with a faint tinge of smoke. It had a subdued and luxurious feel. They sat down on red velvet–covered chairs, in the small lounge area adjacent to the reception desk.

"When did Ms. Nielsen arrive here?" Katie asked.

"Three days ago," the manager replied.

"Was she traveling alone?"

"Yes. She'd booked a fortnight's trip with her husband, but he fell ill before they traveled so she arrived on her own. He was planning to join her later, I believe."

"And did you notice if she saw anyone while here? Made any friends? Did you know what her plans were yesterday?"

The manager sighed.

"She was a little upset that our hotel was so far out of town. I think her husband had made the booking. She seemed to be one of those people who liked being in an urban environment, with everything close by."

"So how did you manage that?" Leblanc asked.

"We called her a cab every time she wanted to go into town, which was often twice a day. The cab company is Island Wheels. They're a small, private company that specializes in hotel transfers. I have already spoken to Irene, who drove her. She said that the first day, she went down to the harbor in the morning and then to the town's main street in the afternoon. The second day, she went into town both times. And yesterday, she stayed at the hotel in the morning and then went to the town's main street at five p.m."

That sounded as if she was planning on doing late afternoon shopping, or perhaps a walk through town and an early dinner, Katie hazarded, wishing she knew more.

"Do you know if she had any plans for the evening? Had she made reservations anywhere? Made any friends? Taken any calls?"

The manager shook her head. "We didn't make any bookings for her apart from the cab transfers."

"Did she tell Irene where she was going?" Leblanc asked.

"No. She didn't tell her in advance about the pick-ups either. She would message when she wanted to come home and send a location pin drop."

Katie sighed. This was a setback, because she could have gone anywhere within Halifax's town center, which was close to the harbor.

"Was she warned about the murders?"

"Yes. We shared a photo of the escaped convict with all our guests and everyone was aware that they should look out for him. But now I believe it wasn't him at all?"

Katie nodded. "Unfortunately, yes," she said.

They were not going to get more information from the hotel.

"Thank you so much. Please get in touch if you think of anything else." Standing up, she handed the manager a card.

Katie was feeling discouraged that they were coming up against more dead ends. But, as they walked out of the hotel, her phone rang.

It was Callum on the line.

"We've got some initial results from the pathologist and forensics," he said. "The shoe prints are a size eleven, and I'll message you the name of the boot brand. It's unfortunately a common one here and available in a lot of stores. But it does indicate that this killer lives locally."

"I see," Katie said.

"We then got some more specific information when the postmortem began."

"What are your findings?" Katie said, quickly turning the call to speaker as they hurried back to the car.

"I'm standing with the pathologist right now. Hold on and you can speak to him."

He handed the phone over, and a deep voice came onto the line. Katie recognized it from her brief chat with him on the island earlier.

"Hi, Agent Winter. I've done the initial exam, and what I've found is that the wound has very jagged edges and distinct entry marks. That wasn't visible in the other victims due to the time that had elapsed, and the damage done by predators. But it's very visible here."

"What could have caused that?" Katie asked.

"It seems to be more than a serrated blade. This looks to be the work of a barbed weapon. I'm certain that it's a large, three-tined fishing spear, because you can actually see the three deep wounds made in two different areas by the tines."

Katie felt encouraged that they had this information.

"So you're sure about that?"

"We'll examine the wounds more closely, but yes, I'm pretty sure. I've seen flesh injuries from fishing spears before and these are identical."

"Any other information?"

"The killer is right-handed. Strong. And there's a slight downward trajectory to the blows, indicating they are made from a height. That also ties in with the shoe size. So the perpetrator is a tall, strong, powerful, right-handed man."

"Thank you," Katie said. She cut the call and turned to Leblanc.

"So we have a picture of our killer."

"He's size eleven and wears local boots, so that points to him being a local himself," Leblanc said.

"And he's not targeting Americans, although the first two victims both happened to be American. He's simply targeting tourists. Any visitors. Male, female. Young, older. American, European."

"Yes," Leblanc said. "It's widened the parameters."

"And thirdly, he's using a three-tined fishing spear."

They sat in the car for a while in silence, thinking about this new information and what it could mean.

"For a start, we could find out more about that fishing spear. It sounds like a distinctive model, with those three tines. The boots might be run of the mill, but perhaps if we look at where the spear is sold, we'll narrow down the options," Katie suggested.

She knew it wouldn't be easy. It would take time, and they still had no idea who the killer was. But at least they now had a clearer picture of the type of person they were searching for.

"The spear's a good starting point," Leblanc agreed. "I'm sure they must be sold down at the harbor. I noticed a fishing shop there. There are probably a few dotted around the area."

"Let's find out more about their customers, and the numbers they sell," Katie decided.

CHAPTER TWENTY ONE

Leblanc headed into the fishing supplies store, feeling optimistic about this new evidence. He hoped the day might be redeemed after the crushing disappointment of the morning.

At least they now had a murder weapon to search for.

A three-tined fishing spear. Heavy-duty, sharp, and lethal. Wielded by a tall, strong, powerful, right-handed man.

He walked into the store, shoulder to shoulder with Katie, and his attention was immediately drawn by the array of spears displayed behind the counter. There were all different types, with different combinations of tines. But all of them looked lethally sharp, with wicked, barbed edges.

The attendant looked at them curiously. Leblanc guessed the two of them did not fit the description of the average fisherman who came in here looking to buy gear.

"Good morning," Leblanc said, walking up to the owner, a fit-looking man in his sixties with a weathered face and a wide smile.

His manner was friendly and open, apparently pleased to see some new faces.

"We're police, investigating the recent crimes," Leblanc said. "Do you have a few minutes to talk to us?"

"Absolutely! I've got time to help the police in any way I can. What can I do for you?"

"We're looking for some information regarding a possible murder weapon."

"The murder weapon?" The man's cheerful expression darkened. "Sure. How can I help? You think he used something we sell?"

"Do you stock any three-tined fishing spears?"

"Only a few," the man said, his eyes widening still further. "Our trident design is for those fishermen who hunt big game fish. Was that—was that the weapon used in those killings?" He sounded incredulous.

"We're following up on all leads," Leblanc said, deciding it was better not to be too specific.

"How many of them do you sell?" Katie asked.

"We probably sell twenty or so in a season."

Too many to track down, Leblanc thought, given that there were probably a couple of other stores in the wider area that they would also need to check.

"Do you keep customer records?" Katie asked.

The man grimaced. "We try to. But the locals don't like giving information, and with the tourists there's not generally a reason to, as they are here for a short time and then gone. I know it's something we should do. But we've not done it so far, and I know the other stores don't either."

"Do you sell more of them to tourists, or locals?" Leblanc asked.

"Definitely to locals. Occasionally, a tourist will buy one, but generally the locals are the ones who do the hunting of the bigger fish. The tourists go for the smaller fish, which is why there's been such an outcry recently about overfishing."

"What outcry is that?" Katie asked. Leblanc could see she was curious.

"You know how it goes. People complain that the food chain is disrupted. If too many of the smaller fish are caught, it means less resources for the bigger fish."

That was interesting to Leblanc. It indicated a potential point of conflict. In fact, it indicated a reason for a local to have a grudge against tourists. Since tourists from all over the globe were being targeted, they needed to consider any recent flashpoints.

"Can you tell us more? Are some locals concerned that this is happening?"

"It's more in summer that you see the tension. That's when the tourists are here and the locals are fishing for their livelihood. It wasn't a good season last year, which has definitely increased the competition over the resources," he explained. "And then there was that incident a few weeks ago. It was a big story in the local media."

"Why?" Katie pressed.

"Well, apparently there was illegal fishing going on. A boat was spotted fishing illegally in a protected area. It looks to have been a big boat, more like a tourist boat than a fishing boat. So that got everyone's back up even more, that one of the locals was allowing this, and that tourists were invading the protected territories."

"That's potentially significant for us," Katie said. "Did they find out who it was?"

"No, they didn't. Which is a shame, because it's not good for the ecosystem. It's not good for the environment. And it really starts to impact the fishermen, because they aren't able to catch the smaller fish themselves."

"And who has been the most outspoken about this?" Katie asked.

"The man who spearheaded the protests was an environmentalist. Name of, let me think now. Josh. Josh something, who does a lot of research and makes a fuss. He's been writing to the papers and the government. He even came in here a while ago to make me sign a petition to protect the fishing territories from 'the depredations of tourists' as he calls it."

"Do you know if there have been any altercations or threats between himself and any of the tourists?"

The man nodded. "I have heard a lot of reports confirming exactly that. Some of the stories are rather shocking. But I would prefer not to repeat them without knowing the full details."

"I understand," Katie sympathized.

"I've remembered his last name. He's called Josh Campbell. And he definitely lives in Nova Scotia, if that's helpful to you in any way."

"It will be. Thank you," Leblanc said.

"He's a bit weird. Always talking about the environment and what's right and wrong and so on. Claims he's an environmentalist, but he's got no qualifications, no formal education that I know of. But then again, I guess you don't need formal education to be concerned about something. You can't blame them for caring about the environment, but some of them go too far, you know? It seems to me that this guy is looking to ban all tourists, not just the ones who fish. He's being too extreme. He wants all visitors off the island."

Leblanc knew that sometimes, the people who were wedded to a cause became enmeshed in extremism. But if this was their killer, it explained why he was targeting all tourists, not just fishermen. Because to him, any tourist now represented a threat.

They headed out and Leblanc turned to Katie.

"This environmentalist. He sounds worth following up?"

"I think we should talk to him," Katie said. "And I'm interested by what the store owner said about blaming all tourists, and being extreme. I think we should check if he has had any run-ins with the police. With that attitude, he might well have."

"It will probably be quickest to call the local office and find out," Leblanc said, getting out his phone.

In a moment, he had dialed and was listening to it ring.

"Good morning, Halifax RCMP," the woman on the other end said.

"Leblanc here from the task force," he said quickly. "I need information."

"Sure. How can we assist?"

"Have you got any records on a local man by the name of Josh Campbell? He's an environmentalist."

"Records? As in personal information? I can look up his address for you. Do you need anything else?"

"Yes. Can you check for any reports of local altercations with tourists, or anything related to his environmentalist work? Perhaps he got into trouble with the police? You might have reports of an arrest, even if charges weren't pressed."

Leblanc waited on the phone, impatiently.

"Yes," the woman said after a pause. "I do have some information. I'm going to call up the reports now."

Leblanc looked excitedly at Katie. The police department was a five-minute drive away. It might be worth reading these reports for themselves if there was more than one, and seeing exactly how far Campbell had gone.

"Can you send us his address and print the reports out for us, and we'll pick them up on the way to go and speak to him?"

"Sure. I will do that," the woman said.

Leblanc disconnected turned to Katie.

"Now that is an interesting new lead," he said.

"It is," she agreed. "The tipping point between fanaticism and violence can often be more of a slippery slope than a balancing act. We need to read up on what Josh Campbell has done, and then see what he has to say about it."

CHAPTER TWENTY TWO

Josh Campbell's home address was a twenty-mile drive out of Halifax, in a rural area to the west of the peninsula. Katie guessed that living in a more remote area of Nova Scotia was in character for a conservationist.

As Leblanc drove, she read through the police reports, which told a disturbing story about this lean, tall and rangy brown-bearded man whose photo and details were on file.

"He sounds like a likable person until you get on his wrong side," Katie noted. "That's why he's avoided any serious charges so far. He seems to be able to turn on the charm and persuade people when he needs to."

"And when the charm is off?" Leblanc asked.

"He began by standing at the harbor entrance and threatening tourists," Katie read. "That was a year ago now. Then the behavior escalated."

"What did he start doing?"

"He smashed the windows of tour buses in the fishing dock area. He was charged with public mischief, but he got off with a warning. He actually used the opportunity to gain more of a following among like-minded locals who are also looking for an outlet for their grievances."

"That's interesting," Leblanc said. Katie knew he was thinking the same way she was. How far had this behavior gone? Especially when backed up by popularity, support, and the feeling he was invulnerable?

"The reports say he was ordered to stay away from the harbor area, but it seems he ignored that and has been going there regularly to harass the tourists."

"Anything else?"

"I've got a report regarding vandalism of a property. The owner, who runs a tour operations company, said the front wall of his property was spray painted. Apparently the message was, 'Attack the Attackers.'"

"That's an escalation. If he's thinking that way, then he might see these murders as fair retribution," Leblanc said thoughtfully.

"And then, finally, he was involved in a bar fight. The details on that are sketchy. It seems everyone was very drunk. But he was definitely threatening tourists. Tourists were involved. He punched one of them, and smashed a bottle and threatened another with the jagged edge, before other patrons put a stop to things."

"And he has escaped charges?" Leblanc sounded incredulous.

"There was fault on both sides in the bar fight, I believe from a quick read-through. Accounts were confused. And they didn't want to prosecute the tourists when the fight was actually managed and contained by the barman and a few of the locals."

"He still sounds like a troublemaker and a man with a serious ax to grind," Leblanc said.

"Agreed. And here's his house."

They had been driving across Nova Scotia into an increasingly remote area. Ahead was a narrow road with a small, neat cottage on the right.

Leblanc pulled over alongside and parked.

"Is he in, do you think?"

Katie was already frowning, because the carport outside the cottage was empty. It was a quarter to ten in the morning. Was he at work? The constable hadn't provided a recorded place of work for this man. Those details were not known to the police, but it seemed he was not at home.

Feeling anxious now that time was ticking by and their suspect was at large, she climbed out of the car and walked up to the wooden front door.

Katie knocked on the brass knocker and listened.

She heard no movement from inside. The silence was absolute, broken only by the birdsong from the trees that clustered thickly nearby.

Leblanc stood by the car. He spread his arms.

"Where now?" he asked.

"I don't know," she replied.

At that moment, she saw a man peering curiously over the bushy hedge that separated this property from the one next door.

Katie walked over to speak to the neighbor.

"We're looking for Mr. Campbell. Do you know where he is?"

The short man in a dull green jacket looked her up and down.

"Are you the police?"

"Yes, we are," Katie said. "We're investigators, looking into the murders."

The neighbor folded his arms. A shifty expression appeared on his face.

"I don't think you should harass Campbell. He's not your guy. He's got nothing to do with any of these killings. He gets unfairly blamed for all sorts of things because he's trying to protect our community's interests."

He stared at Katie stonily. "But anyway, I have no idea where he is."

"Thank you," Katie said, turning away. She was experienced enough to know she had to pick her fights and that pestering this neighbor was not going to get her anywhere at all. This was helping her understand why Campbell had avoided serious police scrutiny so far. He clearly had a lot of support, and people would go out of their way to defend him.

She walked back to the car, aware of the neighbor grinning in a satisfied way as he watched her.

She climbed inside.

"We're not going to get anywhere questioning the neighbors," she said to Leblanc in a low voice. "My feeling is that they might be covering for him. Perhaps they know he's gone out on a mission to try and cause trouble again."

"Given that, perhaps we should try going to the harbor?" Leblanc said. "The main Halifax harbor, where the tourists go, where he's caused trouble before. I'm sure that's where he'd want to target. Perhaps he'll be there."

*

Twenty minutes later, after another, faster drive back through the rural wilds of Nova Scotia, she and Leblanc arrived back at the main harbor.

They parked in the public parking lot, and Katie got out and stared around. This was the biggest harbor. If she was a trouble-making environmentalist, where would she go?

Not down to the fishing boats. Katie guessed that in Campbell's shoes, she would go and haunt the tour buses. That was where she'd look to disrupt and harass. The harbor itself was a big place, and there were a few smaller outlying boat clubs, but the biggest center for tourists, where the city harbor cruises operated from, was clearly marked.

"That way?" she suggested, and Leblanc nodded agreement.

The sea breeze felt cold on their face as they walked across the paved walkway.

The harbor was busy. They passed the tourist information center and then a few of the harbor restaurants, which looked to be doing a good trade.

Katie glanced into the tourist information center, but she didn't see any bearded men there causing trouble. On the left, another road led down to the fishing boats. She could see a couple of men working on them. Down there, it looked peaceful and quiet.

On the right, tour buses were parked. Already, she could see the backs of three minivans and two larger buses, lined up in the parking lot.

Coming from the other side of the buses, she picked up the sound of angry men's voices. There were definitely people shouting there. The sounds resonated through the breezy air, although she couldn't pick up what they were saying.

Katie raised her eyebrows.

Could it be her guess was right, and Campbell had come down to the harbor to make trouble?

Breaking into a jog, she and Leblanc hurried down the curved roadway to see what was going on.

As she rounded the buses, Katie saw her theory had been one hundred percent accurate.

The biggest bus was waiting to leave, but it couldn't, because an angry-looking bearded man was standing in front of it, swinging a golf club with a purposeful air.

The bus driver had climbed out of the bus and was standing on the blacktop facing him, looking distressed. Knots of tourists were watching, looking horrified and intrigued.

"Move, please, sir! Move out of the way! I have to go and make a pickup."

Walking faster, Katie saw that the knot of people was blocking the bus's way out.

In his other hand, Campbell was brandishing a megaphone and as she watched, he began shouting into it.

"You're not going to bring more tourists here! These people are destroying this land and killing this ocean with their greed! I'm not going to allow you to leave. Tell your passengers to stop overfishing the seas. We don't need this. Our locals are suffering!"

"Move, please! Move now!" the driver shouted.

"I won't let you through!" Campbell was calling out.

"I need you to move!" the driver shouted, his voice strained. "I need to get this bus away!"

Seeing that the only choices were a stalemate or a violent showdown, Katie decided to intervene as fast as she could.

She hurried down the roadway and approached the two men.

"Agent Winter and Detective Leblanc. We're from the task force. Perhaps we can help here."

As she moved forward, she assessed Campbell carefully. He looked angry. He looked ready to do something violent. The only good thing was that he didn't seem to have a weapon on his person. His hands were full. One holding the megaphone, one holding the club.

"Campbell?" Katie said. "Josh Campbell?"

He glowered at her. "So someone called the cops on us?" he demanded.

He didn't look likable right now, Katie decided. She'd have to take other people's word about the charming side he showed, which was not in the least apparent now.

"We're here regarding the recent murders. I need to ask you some questions. You need to come in with us."

"Me?" The tall bearded man looked at her with a pugnacious expression. "Why?"

"We understand you've been causing trouble for tourists on a regular basis. I need to confirm your whereabouts and movements at the times of the recent crimes."

"You're calling me a criminal?"

Arrogant to a fault, Katie realized he hadn't moved out of the road. He didn't look like he was going to.

Leblanc, clearly thinking the same, strode forward and seized his arm.

"Come with us, please, Mr. Campbell."

"Don't you touch me!"

With a flash of anger, Campbell wrenched his arm away from Leblanc and took a swipe at him with the golf club.

The metal head bashed into Leblanc's shoulder and he let out a cry of outraged pain. He made a grab for Campbell's other arm but the man jumped back, brandishing the golf club again.

Katie was not going to take a moment more of this than she had to. They'd both endangered themselves enough on this investigation.

She took out her gun and aimed it at the environmentalist.

"Drop that club, or I will shoot," she snapped at him. "And I mean it. If you don't want a bullet in the shoulder, you let that golf club go, now."

He shot her the most poisonous look she'd ever received. But he knew he couldn't argue back. Not against an agent holding a gun and standing out of arm's reach.

Campbell dropped the club and it clattered to the ground.

"You're coming in with us. Handcuff him," she told Leblanc, not moving the gun as he angrily directed Campbell to turn around. There was scattered applause from the watching tourists as the handcuffs clamped shut on his wrists.

This guy was used to getting away with whatever he felt like doing. He was arrogant, entitled, and played by his own rules, believing he'd never get into trouble. Had his escalating agenda included murder?

Katie couldn't wait to get him into the police department and find out.

CHAPTER TWENTY THREE

"What's going on there?" The man Garrison was talking to, a slightly overweight, forty-something man with soft hands and office pallor, had turned curiously to look at the commotion down by the tour buses.

"Ah, that's our local environmentalist at work," Garrison reassured him smoothly, giving him a conspiratorial grin. "That man's forever getting involved in preventing the big tour boats from going out. He is down there at least twice a week, blocking the buses and trying to create a disturbance. I've actually seen it become a photo opportunity. People have even videoed him in the past."

They were standing about a hundred yards away, closer to the harbor. It was a bright morning with barely a breath of wind. The harbor was crowded with boats, fishing boats and pleasure boats. Tourists were scattered around. Locals were briskly going about their business.

"Well, I'm glad I'm not going out on a big boat," the man said. "I would find that delay very annoying. I wish there was time to go out on the water though. It looks wonderful."

Garrison nodded, smiling.

"I've been sailing out of this harbor for more than a decade, and I can tell you, mornings like this are something special. It's magical being out at sea when it's this still."

"Yes, I can believe that," the man said, looking yearningly out at the wavelets.

"I'm sorry," Garrison said warmly. "We've been chatting for a while already and I haven't even asked you your name."

"My name? I'm Pete Jackson."

"Garrison."

He held his hand out and the tourist shook it.

"So what brings you to this part of the world, Pete?" he asked.

"I'm a finance manager for an insurance firm in New Jersey. I'm over here on a conference. I arrived early and decided to see some sights before work starts. After that, the inside of the hotel is all I'll see from lunch time onward. Meetings, events, hopefully some dinners."

Garrison nodded. "Whereabouts are you staying?"

"At the Marriott."

"Nice place. It's not far from here, if I recall?"

"No, it's close by. I took a walk along the boardwalk. It's very scenic and busier than I expected. I'd like to go further, but don't have the time now."

Garrison noticed he was sweating lightly. This was not a fit man. Was it a lack of time or fitness that was keeping him from going further? he wondered briefly, feeling amused.

He knew it was important to ask the man about himself. People automatically built a relationship of trust when they talked about themselves.

Plus, in one part of his mind at least, he was genuinely interested. It was always fascinating to learn about other people, their lives, their experiences. Even if, most times, their lives ended with a very special experience, personalized by him.

"So you work in finance. How interesting. What do you deal with?"

"Credit risk. I run the models that determine credit ratings."

Garrison nodded. "That must be demanding work."

"Well, a lot of people don't find numbers fascinating," Jackson admitted. "But someone has to do it, right? It pays the bills."

"But it's not really your passion?" Garrison surmised.

"Is it anyone's passion?" Jackson asked. "I love getting paid, but the job itself—it's not a passion. Just a way to make money."

"I see." Garrison nodded. "So what's your passion, then?"

Jackson laughed. "Well, I don't know if I have one."

"Sure you do," Garrison said. "It may not be your job, but it's something. You like something. Maybe it's a sport, like sailing?"

It wasn't walking, that was for sure, he thought again, laughing inwardly.

"I do love sailing." Jackson nodded. "I've sailed in the past, but now I'm too busy with work to go out on the water. I miss it."

The man looked down at his watch and then back at the sea, where the boats were still at anchor.

"I wish there was time to book a tour," he said yearningly.

"Look, I wasn't planning on going out this morning," Garrison said. "I was planning on doing some chores. But the boat's here, and if you'd like to go for a couple of hours, I'll take you. I know what it's like to love sailing and not be able to get out. There are some small islands nearby here that are very picturesque." He nodded at Pete Jackson reassuringly. He knew it was important not to seem too eager. And truthfully he wasn't. It was always the victims' choice. Every step of the way.

Jackson looked at his watch again. "I'm not sure. We have registration at twelve-thirty."

Garrison smiled. "I know the waters. We can be back in time for you to make it easily. There's a two-hour route I do with guests that takes you to some of the best places. And it's quarter past ten now."

Garrison glanced around. The protest had cleared. Out of the corner of his eye, although he'd been focused on Jackson and not really taking note, he thought he'd seen the cops arrive. At any rate, this time the environmentalist had been dragged away.

That was good. He was an interfering man, always making trouble and trying to pry. That was something Garrison detested, for his own reasons of course. The less attention and focus on the harbor, the less police presence, the happier he was.

"Well, if you're sure that won't be a problem," Jackson said, sounding relieved.

"Not at all." Garrison smiled. I'm a very experienced sailor, and the route is a good one. No problems."

"Okay then." Jackson nodded. He took his wallet out. "How much?" he said dubiously. He was holding his wallet tightly as if he wasn't keen to open it up at all. Watching his body language, Garrison decided he was likely to go for a deal.

"I don't usually give this price for tourists on their own. But for you, it'll be just fifty dollars for our two-hour exclusive."

The man handed over the cash. Then they turned and strolled along the quay, heading for Garrison's boat. He noted Jackson began breathing hard from the slight exertion.

"Do you live here all year round?" Jackson asked.

"I'm lucky enough to be a local here, yes. The winters are harsh, I will admit. But the summers make up for it and the sailing is unsurpassed."

"And do you run tours full time?"

Garrison shrugged. "When I can, yes. I enjoy showing people around. It's a beautiful area. And the ocean here is so special."

"And when you're not running tours?"

Garrison smiled. "This might sound crazy to you. But I'm an actor."

"An actor? Like, in the movies?" Jackson asked, surprised.

Garrison shook his head. "No, no. Small, local productions only. I specialize in those. You could call it my passion. It's very exciting, I find, to step into the skin of another character and pretend to be someone else."

"You're an interesting man," Jackson said admiringly.

"And you're an interesting guy yourself," Garrison said, smiling.

They reached the marina and he led the way onto the floating dock. His boat was moored in its slip, a thirty-foot cabin cruiser called *The Osprey*.

Jackson examined the boat admiringly. It was perfectly clean, shiny and obviously well-maintained. Garrison could see him being seduced by the boat's immaculate exterior. The gleaming yellow wheelhouse and the tubular, gunmetal-gray rails.

"She's a beauty," Jackson said.

"I know," Garrison said, with a grin.

So much for the seduction. It had never been an issue. Jackson was just another victim.

They stepped onto the boat and Jackson paused for a second, looking about him. He seemed quite happy on the boat. He was clearly an experienced sailor and didn't need to be shown the ropes. Garrison was relieved. It was important to be assured of the victim's comfort.

That way he was more likely to relax and follow Garrison's lead. That was something he'd learned during his long career.

Otherwise, his victims might be more inclined to fight back too early. And he didn't want that. Not ever. It was much easier if they were relaxed and confident, right up until the big reveal.

Garrison stepped off the boat again once he was sure Jackson was comfortably seated. He loosened the mooring ropes and shoved the bow out of its slip, then hopped in and started the engine.

He was looking forward to the next couple of hours. They were going to be fun.

CHAPTER TWENTY FOUR

What a deal he'd gotten, Pete Jackson thought, feeling a sense of triumph as the boat headed out on the water. This was one for the books. Fifty dollars for a two-hour exclusive? Wait till the other guys heard. He'd been lucky, coming down to the harbor early.

The tour was proving even better than he'd expected. This was a fantastic boat, and Garrison obviously knew the local waters well. He was a great skipper.

"Okay," Garrison said, as they reached the harbor limits. "We're clear. We'll open up the throttle now."

He moved forward and the engine roared to life. Jackson felt the boat pick up speed, the water rushing along the sides and the bow lifting gracefully. He loved it. The ocean breeze on his face, the sun overhead, and the hull of the boat slicing through the sea, and all for fifty dollars!

A knockdown price.

For a moment, Jackson seriously wondered if he should tip this guy.

He wasn't a tipper. He didn't believe in it. People should work for their salary and not expect more. He was proud that in the past twenty years, he'd never left a tip. Not for anyone. Not for the waiters, or the barmen, or his barber, or the parking attendants. But it showed how warm his mood was, that the thought actually occurred to him. He was surprised by it.

Garrison took them along the coastline for a few minutes, then turned and headed farther out to sea. He was a skilled sailor. The boat handled like a dream.

He watched the boat cut through the waves, feeling a sense of powerful exhilaration. This was one of the finest days he'd ever experienced.

"Want to steer for a while?" Garrison asked him.

Jackson shook his head. "No thanks. I'll watch you. I'm enjoying it up here."

"Okay." Garrison nodded.

They continued along at a steady pace, and then Garrison throttled back.

"We're nearly there," Garrison said, pointing ahead of them. "This is well worth seeing."

Jackson looked to where he was indicating. He could see a small island. Not big, about a mile long, he reckoned, and deeply wooded, but with a good-sized hill at the center of it.

A lighthouse stood on the rocky beach. It looked like it was abandoned.

"This is a great spot for photos," Garrison explained. He glanced sidelong at Jackson. "We're not really allowed to go on the island. The lighthouse is off limits. But if you want, seeing it's a private tour, we can moor the boat here and take a walk up the beach. Going inside that lighthouse is quite fascinating."

"Yes, yes. I can see that it would be." Jackson stared at it eagerly.

"It's your choice. I guess the question I need to ask you is, do you want to go into an off-limits area? Or would you rather stick to the rules?" He grinned at Jackson.

"Will this cost any more?" Jackson asked, suddenly thinking that this man was looking to squeeze more money out of him.

"It's included in the price."

"Then I guess I want to break the rules," Jackson said. "Let's go see this lighthouse. If it's off-limits, it makes it even more interesting."

He folded his arms, leaning back against the rail, feeling super stoked with himself as Garrison maneuvered the boat expertly close to the tumbledown wooden pier.

Jackson quickly stepped across and walked down the weathered, slimy boards.

He headed up the beach, the rocks and pebbles scrunching under his expensive shoes, being careful to avoid the foaming wavelets that rushed up. He didn't want to get his pants legs wet, with the conference starting soon.

It was a fair walk to the lighthouse. He guessed it was impossible to moor a boat closer because of the rocks. This coastline was very rocky and craggy. No wonder it made for such great photos. He couldn't wait to take a selfie of himself outside the forbidden lighthouse.

He was smiling from ear to ear as he climbed the small hill, thinking how cool this all was. A private tour of a forbidden lighthouse, for just fifty dollars.

Jackson stopped for a second, distracted by the view. The sea stretched out in every direction, a patchwork of blues and greens, pockmarked with islands, and with the mainland at the horizon. Wow. He had to make sure he got a good shot of this. The island was almost deserted. A few seagulls circled it, but apart from that, there was no life to be seen.

Garrison was walking behind him.

"This place is so remote," Jackson said. "I'm surprised it hasn't been discovered by photographers."

"There are a few photographers who come here," Garrison said. "But like I said, it's officially protected territory."

Jackson turned and looked up at the lighthouse. It was falling into disrepair. Some of the windows were broken and the paint was peeling. Still, it looked awesome.

"Do we get to go inside?" he asked, striding up to the door.

"Just wait a moment."

To Jackson's surprise, Garrison shouldered ahead of him. It was almost rude, the way he suddenly pushed in front of him as they reached the lighthouse door.

Jackson felt miffed. It was as if his demeanor had changed. He didn't seem like the friendly guy he was back in the harbor. Maybe he was regretting the discounted tour he'd offered, but Jackson wasn't paying him a cent more. And no way was he tipping him, now that he'd pushed past him like that. Not that tipping had actually ever been on the cards, but still.

Garrison took hold of the door and opened it a foot or so. There was an unpleasant scream of hinges.

He leaned inside.

Jackson frowned. What was he doing? Checking for something? He wasn't opening up, that was for sure.

Then Garrison turned around and Jackson saw, to his utter astonishment, the man was holding something. Brandishing it high in the air.

Something long and heavy, silvery and sharp, with a vicious, barbed head that was aimed directly at him.

He gasped at the expression on Garrison's face; one of fierce, evil joy. This man was not joking. This was not a prank. Intent burned in his eyes.

His mind staggered with shock as he tried to take in the truth; that this person had lured him out here to spear him to death with this awful-looking implement.

The man stared at him triumphantly.

"Run," he whispered.

Jackson let out a mewl of pure terror. And then, with a speed that surprised him, he took off along the coastline, not in the direction of the boat but the other way, sprinting as fast as he possibly could, wanted to get away, to outrun the man, even though he knew Garrison's legs were longer and more powerful, and even now he could hear him thudding along behind.

He couldn't outrun him. He didn't have the stamina. But he had to try and save his own damned life.

The footsteps were closer.

Crunch, crunch, implacably catching up to him over the rocks.

He wanted to look over his shoulder, but he didn't dare. That would slow him down, and he knew if he slowed, he'd be dead.

He could hear the man's breathing behind him, could hear his rapid footsteps, could hear the harsh, wanton panting of his pursuer.

He must be swinging that terrible implement, Jackson thought. The thought made him run even faster.

At that moment, his foot twisted, and he stumbled over a rock. Then he yelled as he felt the terrible, cutting blow of the fishing spear pierce his shoulder.

Pain lanced through him, but the adrenaline it brought with him gave him the strength to turn and fight.

He swung around and shoved the man with all his might as he was raising the spear again.

Victory.

Garrison slipped back, falling down into a rocky crevasse with a cry.

Jackson couldn't waste any time. Even though his lungs were burning and his heart banging in his chest he had to try and get away now, to use this lead.

And he could!

There was a tourist boat ahead, out on the sea. He could see it in the distance.

His shoulder was burning and he could feel blood soaking his shirt, but the wound was not fatal. He could still make it. He plunged along the shoreline, shouting and waving.

"Help!" he cried. "Help me!"

Had they seen him? The entire deck was lined with tourists all looking at the island. They must have seen him.

"Help!" he cried again.

But at that moment, Jackson felt a fresh spurt of pain. This one didn't come from his shoulder. It came from the front left side of his chest. He sank to his knees, feeling suddenly weak. It was too late. At this moment, his heart had given up on him. That was what it must be.

Sprawling down on the rocky beach, he could only watch as the world around him turned gray, and then dark.

From behind him, he heard an incredulous chuckle.

"Poor man," Garrison called, but Jackson didn't know if he was really hearing the words or just imagining them. "Now that really is bad luck!"

CHAPTER TWENTY FIVE

"Get into the car, Mr. Campbell," Katie said to the aggressive environmentalist, as they approached the police vehicle. Leblanc was keeping a tight hold of his cuffed hands, but she saw the fight had gone out of him—for now. She had experience with people like this. They didn't stay down for long. She was sure that questioning this man would not be an easy process, but she was determined to get the truth out of him.

Leblanc hustled him over to the car and Katie glanced back, seeing the tour bus driver get back inside his vehicle and drive away looking relieved.

Beyond, the harbor looked scenic and peaceful. It was a beautiful morning. The blue waters and colorful boats gave it a postcard charm. The harbor was already busy, with people coming and going.

These were people who had every right to go about their business and help tourists enjoy the area without being harassed, stopped, or murdered. Resolve hardened inside Katie to bring the offender to justice as soon as she possibly could.

She climbed inside the car and slammed the door.

"Where are you taking me?" Campbell asked from the back. Leblanc was sitting beside him. They were taking no chances with this man.

"You're going to the nearest RCMP office for questioning," Katie said.

Glancing into the mirror, she saw Campbell's face set.

"I'm a Canadian citizen," he said, "and I want to contact a lawyer."

"You're not under arrest," Katie said. "Not yet."

She pulled into the flow of traffic, heading toward downtown.

"Not yet? Are you planning to charge me with something?" Campbell asked.

"You assaulted an officer of the law. That, on its own, carries jail time. But it's not what we're most interested in," Katie enlightened him.

"What are you most interested in?" Now Campbell's voice was wary.

"We're most interested in your recent movements. Over the past couple of days. I'm going to need a full, complete account of how and where you spent your time. So I suggest you start trying to remember so we don't waste time once we're interrogating you," Katie snapped.

"But I didn't do anything," he said, suddenly sounding meek and afraid.

"That remains to be seen," Katie shot back.

Campbell cleared his throat. "I think it's pretty clear what you're getting at. You think I killed the tourists. But I didn't."

"Then you have nothing to worry about, do you?" Katie said.

Campbell didn't answer.

They reached the RCMP building, and Katie parked outside.

She walked around to the back of the car and opened up. Flanking Campbell, she and Leblanc escorted him inside.

They headed straight for the interview room and Leblanc got the environmentalist into a chair.

He stared at them, and now the anger on his face was replaced with a quizzical concern as he stared around the small room, warm and stuffy, with its mirrored window and wooden desk that was bare apart from a notebook and a tape recorder.

Katie pressed the button to record the interview.

"Officers, I know you have the wrong guy," he said. There was warmth in his tone that she hadn't expected to be there. Finally Katie realized she was seeing his charming side.

The side that he would use to try to manipulate people into doing what he wanted, she guessed. To lure people out on a boat, charm would be needed. So this wasn't persuading her he was innocent. In fact, the opposite.

"I'm not the one you should be investigating," he pleaded.

"Let's talk about your movements," Katie said, sitting down across from him while Leblanc undid his cuffs.

"Within the past forty-eight hours," Leblanc added.

"Absolutely. I can see why you need that information. But truly, you're looking in the wrong direction. I know you probably think I'm a violent man. A killer, even. But what you don't realize is that I'm just looking to speak up for those who can't. Fish can't talk. They can't say you're destroying my environment. Sea creatures have no voice. We have to protest for them and that's what I do. If you ask me, you should be looking at the tour boats," he said, clearly warming to his topic.

"Don't worry, we will," Katie said. "Right now, though, we need an account of your movements and whereabouts."

But it seemed Campbell wasn't yet ready to start giving that information.

"The truth is, and I admit this without any shame, I'm just not violent. I care deeply about animals. That's why I do what I do. I do my best to help them. So that's why I need you to understand I didn't kill those tourists. I know I have a reputation and it's one that I never earned. I'm not a killer. I'm not a violent man. But the tour boats are out of control. There are licensed boats. Unlicensed boats. There are people who'll go out there and break the laws in any way they can, just to give tourists a thrill. The thrill of destroying things nature has taken eons to build. The thrill of fishing in protected areas. They're destroying the habitat. They're destroying the work we have done, the work we are trying to achieve. If you want to know who murdered the tourists, you need to look at the people who are breaking the environmental laws. And I mean that in all honesty."

He smiled.

Katie had to admit it was an appealing, charismatic smile.

"I appreciate your argument. But you're overlooking the fact you, too, have broken the law. Just in different ways."

"Point taken," he agreed.

"But Mr. Campbell, this is not why you are here. Where have you been in the last two days?"

He nodded. "I'm sorry for wasting your time, but I wanted to explain my thinking to you. As for my movements, I'll tell you. This morning, I was at the harbor from approximately nine a.m. First I met with the harbormaster. He was rude to me as always and wouldn't tell me if the tour boats and tour buses were all properly registered. So I stood in front of one to get his attention, but you saw me first."

"Go on," Katie said.

"Yesterday, I was out of town. I sailed across to Prince Edward Island the day before for a meeting in Charlottetown. It's a group of environmentalists that get together every few months to discuss issues. I got there in the evening the day before yesterday. We had drinks and dinner at the hotel. Then yesterday morning, we had our meeting. We wrapped up after lunch, and I sailed back again. I moored my boat in the harbor at about six p.m. You can check that with the harbormaster. Trust me, they keep an eye on my comings and goings."

"The hotel reservation. Do you have proof?"

Katie was stunned by the fact this man had not even been in Nova Scotia at the time of the recent killings. No way could he have committed the crime if his alibi held up.

"Of course I do. Here's my phone." He opened it and slid it across the table. "All the messages are there. The hotel bookings were done by email. I even got an electronic notification when I moored in Charlottetown. Take your time. I have nothing to hide. I could have told you earlier, but I really wanted you to understand where I was coming from and the importance of my work."

He smiled again.

Katie felt flattened by this bombshell as she scrolled through the phone. It was obvious that he was telling the truth. The chain of evidence was far too complex for him to have hastily fabricated it.

He was not their man.

And at that moment, her phone buzzed.

"Excuse me," she said, getting up and hurrying outside when she saw Scott on the line.

"Kate, where are you?" Scott's voice was brittle and stressed.

"Questioning a suspect. We've just confirmed his alibi," she said with a twist of her stomach, wondering what news he was calling to bring. Sure enough, his next words confirmed her fears.

"There's just been another murder. A victim has been found on one of the islands close to Halifax, near an abandoned lighthouse. This is recent. Very recent. As in, witnesses watched him die."

Now, Katie felt despair descend.

While they had been bringing Campbell in, the killer had been at work. For all she knew, she'd been staring right at him when she took a look around the harbor.

"We're on our way there," she told her boss. "We'll get to the scene immediately. I won't let this happen again. Whatever it takes, we're going to find him this time."

CHAPTER TWENTY SIX

Katie felt pummeled by self-blame as she and Leblanc climbed off the speedboat and headed over to the latest crime scene, while Callum moored the boat on the rocky beach.

The island was small and scenic, with the abandoned lighthouse a compelling focal point. In the morning sun, it looked clean and bright.

But it had been the site of another kill. Approaching the slumped body inside the crime scene tape being strung up, she simply could not comprehend that they had been so close to him, but were now still so far behind.

"I can't believe this has happened again," she muttered to Leblanc.

They had failed. They were chasing shadows, rushing off in the wrong direction, and the killer was still two steps ahead. Still unknown. Still picking his victims off with impunity.

"We were there. Right there. At the harbor. Taking in the wrong guy," he said, his voice bitter.

Katie's phone rang again. It was Scott on the line once more.

"Are you on the scene yet?" he demanded.

"We just got here," Katie said.

"I am taking big strain with this. The premier of Nova Scotia wants an urgent meeting with me. I'm going to have to take the next plane out there and hopefully arrive later this afternoon. They are desperate for answers. This is impacting hugely on their tourism, and right at the start of the season, the timing could not be worse."

"I understand," Katie said grimly.

"I don't want to pull the other task force members off of their case, because they're busy handling a series of violent cash-in-transit heists near the Washington State border, but if I have to, I will."

"We'll try our best," Katie protested, but Scott continued harshly. "I could probably spare Clark tomorrow morning. If we haven't had results by then, I'll send him."

The words burned Katie. She knew Scott just wanted this solved, and that he was under severe pressure, but the take-home message that seared into her mind was that she and Leblanc were not good enough.

And there was no way she could argue back. They were not good enough. The case was unsolved and the body count was piling up.

"We'll do our best. I will report back as soon as I can," she said.

Katie paced over to the scene, where the coroner was already at work.

"Tourists on a passing ship saw the victim stumbling along the beach, waving his arms and shouting for help," Callum explained, as he headed to the scene. He sounded as frustrated as they felt.

"What happened? Did he succumb to his injuries? Did they see any sign of the killer?"

Callum shook his head. "The first reports we received were of a lone tourist who was stranded. By the time the boat sailed in closer, there was no sign of anyone else and the man had collapsed. The skipper said initially they'd thought he was just left behind, that he'd been with another group and they had sailed off without him. And that was why he was calling for help. Because he was all on his own. So they altered course to fetch him. Then, when a few of them looked closer, they realized he was in a panic and at that stage they sped up. But then, in front of all of them, he collapsed."

"I see," Katie said, feeling exquisite frustration.

"It was only when they disembarked that they realized the man was badly injured and that this might have been a failed attempt at murder. The skipper called us immediately, got everyone off the island, and immediately sailed around the perimeter in search of the killer. But he said there were no other boats to be seen. So he must have fled."

Katie shook her head, feeling sick.

She saw the trail of footprints. Walking back, she could see two sets of prints on the swathe of sand between the rocks. She recognized the boot prints, their tread unmistakable. The killer had been here, pursuing his target. The man had run and he'd been chased, but he'd gotten far enough away to shout for help.

Seeing the ship, she imagined the killer must have fled.

They had been within minutes of learning the man's identity. But the victim had died.

"Who is he?" she asked.

"Pete Jackson. We saw a hotel room card from the Marriott in his pocket and called them. He's part of a conference. They confirmed he checked in this morning and then went down to the harbor."

"And how did he die? Did he succumb to the injury?" Katie asked, turning to the coroner who was busy with his examination.

"Now, this is interesting," the man muttered from behind his mask.

"What?" Katie said.

"This man was hit in the shoulder. That's not the killer's usual MO. The previous victims have been struck hard in the back. So something happened. Perhaps he was too fast in getting away. But the blow wasn't lethal. I doubt it killed him. You can see the three points clearly, and it bled a lot, but it's unlikely to have been a fatal wound."

"So what killed him?" Katie asked.

"I'm guessing he had a heart attack. That would tie in with what the tourists saw, how he was shouting and waving and he then suddenly collapsed. A couple of them thought he might have gripped his chest as he fell. Probably the effort of fleeing and the stress of the attack precipitated some sort of fatal event."

This was just unbelievable. The victim had escaped the killer, only to perish as a result of his own efforts. Were they going to be forever unlucky on this case?

Katie was beginning to think so.

She stared at the two sets of footprints. She imagined the victim sprinting along the beach, watching over his shoulder as the killer kept pace with him. His heart accelerating. Triggering the event that had killed him even as he tried to save himself.

Bad luck was haunting them here, for sure.

But then she thought again. She drew on the inner strength, the core of toughness that she'd developed at the age of sixteen when her own parents had turned their backs on her, leaving her to handle the disappearance of her twin after the kayaking accident, as well as their anger and blame, all on her own.

She had coped with that and she could cope with this.

What she needed to do now was focus her mind on what they could learn from this, rather than what they could not.

Maybe this was not an unlucky catastrophe, and maybe there was in fact a significant amount of new information that could be taken away from this crime scene.

The events leading up to it were where she saw an opportunity for further facts to be deduced. The cogs of her mind began to turn, processing how this must have played out. And suddenly, she felt more encouraged.

"Leblanc, we need to work with what we have. And maybe, thanks to this, we have enough now."

He frowned. "You think? What do we have? It sure doesn't feel like we have much at all."

"This victim was recently arrived. The hotel staff observed that he walked down to the harbor. I imagine that most of the guests do exactly that on fine days."

"Yes. It would be the obvious place for someone new in town, waiting for a conference to start," Leblanc agreed.

"So the killer must have been basing himself down there. Pete Jackson found him. It wasn't the other way around."

"Agreed. No other way he could have organized that meet-up so quickly," Leblanc agreed.

"Therefore, he has a boat. A boat that is available and ready to use, to lure the victims aboard. And which must be at Halifax harbor, or at any rate it was this morning, because that is where the latest victim was taken from. I'm guessing it's permanently berthed there. It's by far the easiest place to find tourists."

"Okay," Leblanc said, but he sounded doubtful.

"And that means he's a boat skipper. That's how he gets his victims."

Leblanc shook his head. "But the previous victim was taken after a town drop-off. Remember what the hotel told us. Heidi Nielsen called a cab service to take her into town."

"It's a small town. The harbor is only a few blocks away from downtown. She could have strolled down there. Maybe he was on the hunt offering sunset cruises."

Leblanc sighed impatiently. "There was no sunset that day. It was a hideous evening."

"Well, maybe she booked it earlier, or set it up the day before, and decided to honor the booking regardless. At any rate we need to explore this theory."

"Yes. We do. But where to start?" Leblanc asked.

Katie thought for a moment. What route would give them the most effective, and fast, answers?

"Let's start with the harbormaster," she said. "He seems to know who's who. Remember what Campbell told us, that he knew as soon as Campbell entered the harbor?"

"So he runs a tight ship." Leblanc sounded pleased by his analogy.

"Exactly," Katie said. "He will know which tour operators work from this harbor and are here most often. He'll know the troublemakers and the problem individuals. Let's go and speak to him and ask him, in his opinion, which of them we should be investigating most urgently."

CHAPTER TWENTY SEVEN

The harbormaster was a young, energetic-looking man with a blond beard and a can-do attitude that Leblanc immediately liked. He was sitting in a tiny second-floor office, with windows on two sides overlooking the Halifax harbor.

"Craig Syndercombe? Leblanc asked, tapping on the door before walking in, with Katie close behind.

"Yes. That's me. They told me you were on your way." Immediately, the man jumped up from his laptop. "How can I help? Believe me, I'm keen. At the moment I'm processing floods of cancellations. I've taken fifteen calls already this morning asking for status updates and what I'm planning to do to keep visitors safe. They're demanding that security on site gets improved. The problem is that we have no idea where to start, because we don't know enough about why this is happening. I've even requested a personal meeting with the local police on site, but they told me they are so busy, the earliest they can see me is Wednesday."

The harbormaster was clearly distressed by the amount of business his tour operators were losing. And Leblanc was encouraged that he seemed like a hands-on guy.

"From what we've seen so far, it looks like the killer is operating from this harbor. He must have taken the most recent victim out on a boat this morning after the victim checked in at the Marriott."

The harbormaster paled.

"Seriously?"

"Yes. The recent incident has confirmed this."

"That's just such a shock. Here? From here?" He stared out the window, frowning incredulously.

"We need to urgently track down who could have been involved. This victim arrived here just a couple of hours ago. He clearly went out on a tour, most likely alone. So who did he go with? That's what we're asking ourselves and where we thought you could help."

"We don't keep track of everyone's comings and goings, but this was a fine morning and I saw a lot of the boat skippers out early. Of course, we do have a log of all the boats that stay at this harbor. There are a few different boat yards, and well over a hundred boats, so it's not really going to help you. How can we narrow it down?" he asked.

"We need to focus on the main area where the city harbor cruises operate from, because that's closest to the hotel. There wouldn't have been time for him to walk further or find a smaller boat yard."

"Yes. The others are further away. The main one is definitely the most popular destination for hotel residents."

"Then, within there, we need to look at any recent incidents. Any skipper who has had issues with tourists, or who's had a lot of complaints, or who's stepped out of line. Perhaps some people have been fined or had the police involved? Who are the troublemakers?"

"I see. Yes, we do have an incident book that we keep. Would it help if I looked back through that?"

"Yes, it would."

"Why don't you take a seat while I get it? What was the victim's name?"

"Pete Jackson."

"And you don't know anything more? The hotel didn't book the tour for him? They often do."

"Not this time. That's where we need your help."

"Okay. Take a seat. I'll be right back."

Leblanc sat down next to Katie and waited.

The harbormaster was back in about two minutes with a ledger.

"We record everything here. Even the smallest incidents. I guess it's part of my job to keep track of the commercial people who work from here. I'm responsible for policing and harbor issues."

"I understand."

Leblanc and Katie each took a seat at the desk and started looking down the list of entries.

"The most recent entry is this morning. It goes back from there," Syndercombe explained.

"And what serious incidents stand out for you?" Leblanc asked, hoping to provide more clarity on this very detailed list. "Specifically, those involving tourists being abused or treated in a negative way."

Syndercombe nodded, paging through. "You see both sides here. There are complaints and incidents from tour operators and from tourists. I treat both equally seriously. Tourists deserve the same respect as the locals."

"Absolutely."

“There was one report I filed a couple of weeks ago. It was an allegation that a tour operator had behaved inappropriately with a tourist. I looked into it. But it turned out that the tourist, who was a woman, had been very drunk. She’d put herself in an embarrassing situation, and then made a scene when she realized what she’d done.”

“Right.”

“So, I had to conclude that there was no case to answer there.”

“Any others?” Leblanc asked.

We recently had an episode where a tour operator was accused of being abusive to a tourist. We were able to clear him. The trouble was that he was too quick to react when the passenger made a complaint. He was quite prickly to the tourist, so I had to give him a warning. He was very apologetic about it and had no prior record of any trouble.”

“Anything else?” Katie asked. Leblanc agreed that this incident didn’t seem serious enough.

“Here’s the one that really made waves, a month or so ago.” He looked at the page. “A married couple were taken out on a sunset cruise. The husband was left off shore by himself on a small island, miles out to sea, for a few hours. It looked like there must have been more to the situation, but the skipper couldn’t explain his side adequately, and the woman swore it was deliberately done and that he’d intended to cause her husband harm and trauma. So I reported him.”

Leblanc exchanged a glance with Katie. This sounded like an incident that could possibly have been a springboard.

“Is he still operating here?”

“Yes. He had to pay a fine, but he was allowed to continue.”

“And who is he?”

“His name is Ryker Fraser. He has a regular berth here. I’ll show you.”

The harbormaster stood up and, looking as if he was pleased to be getting on his feet, hurried downstairs. Leblanc followed him, feeling positive about this new lead.

Syndercombe strode along the paving, past ranks of boats.

“His is at the end of the line. It’s white, with a green stripe around it.”

He stopped, shaded his eyes.

“He doesn’t seem to be there,” he said.

Frowning, he walked on to the neighboring berth, where a dark-haired skipper was preparing his boat.

"Morning, Heath. Where's Fraser?" he asked.

The man shrugged. "He's been busy this morning. I saw him go out with a tourist a couple of hours ago, and he's just left with another."

"Did you see the first tourist?" Leblanc asked.

"It was a man. Short, plump, maybe forty years old? More than that I can't say," Heath explained.

Leblanc felt his insides clench. He looked at Katie, seeing his feelings reflected in her eyes. This timeframe coincided perfectly with the killing, and the description of the first tourist was very similar to the victim. They needed to find Fraser urgently. Every moment now represented potential danger for the new person on his boat.

"Do you have any idea where he went?" Leblanc asked.

Heath tapped his fingers on the shiny rail of his boat.

"He probably did the short circular route. That's where we often go when we only have one guest."

Syndercombe glanced at the small speedboat that was tethered next to the skipper's larger boat.

"We need a favor. We're following an urgent lead. Can we borrow that for a while?"

"Of course. I need it back by two p.m."

"We'll have it back by then."

Clearly anxious to help, the harbormaster strode to the pier and climbed into the speedboat, beckoning Katie and Leblanc to join him.

Just a few moments later, they were roaring out to sea, spray foaming over the boat's prow.

Leblanc's mouth felt dry, and his heart was thumping. All the evidence was pointing to the fact that Ryker Fraser was their man. He had a history of negative behavior that involved tourists, and also involved the uninhabited islands. And his movements today coincided exactly with the pattern they were looking for.

"Do you know him well?" Leblanc shouted to Syndercombe above the sound of the water churning beneath them.

"Yes, I do," the harbormaster shouted back.

"What's he like?"

"I wouldn't use the word 'what'—it's more like 'who.' Fraser is the local renegade. He's retired military. His wife left him, so he lives alone in a rented flat. He's very friendly on the surface, but underneath, he's very bitter. I've known him for a few years now. He's not an easy person."

Leblanc gripped the gunwales tightly. He felt as if he and Katie were racing to a crime scene. And his deepest fear was that they were. What if they arrived too late to prevent another death?

"Usually, the skippers stop off at one of the islands just for photos. I'm going to check all the ones along this route," Syndercombe said. "I'll look in the less likely mooring spots as well as the more popular ones. Just in case."

Leblanc could tell he was thinking along the right lines.

The first island they skirted was empty. No boats were moored on its shores. The second island, a hundred yards further, was tiny, little more than a rock in the sea, with cold waves lashing it.

The boat scudded over the waves. They sailed in silence. Each of them was surveying the landscape continually. The cold breeze was making Leblanc's eyes water.

And then, suddenly, a shape on the horizon materialized into what they needed.

Moored in a secluded, rocky, natural harbor on a small, thickly forested island, was a bright white boat with a distinctive green stripe.

"He's there!" Leblanc pointed. He glanced at Katie, seeing her face set and determined.

"So he is," Syndercombe said.

Throttling the speedboat to its maximum, he sped toward the island.

Leblanc gripped the hull of the motorboat as they neared Fraser's vessel. What was he up to on that island with one lone tourist? Was he on the boat at all? If this was his typical MO, he would not be on the boat but would already have walked deeper into the island, ready to play out the twisted scene that brought him his murderous pleasure.

Were they going to be in time to stop him, to prevent him from killing again?

Syndercombe slowed the boat as they neared, so they could see if there was anyone aboard.

Leblanc stood up to scan the green-striped boat, which was rocking gently in the water. He saw nobody on board.

But he gasped as he saw a long, heavy fishing spear, placed in a rack at the front of the boat. Narrowing his eyes, he saw it had three barbed tines.

"Look at that," Leblanc murmured to Katie.

"He's not in the boat. He and this tourist must have gone for a hike," Syndercombe said.

"We need to find them," Leblanc said. At this point, he knew that every moment literally counted.

"Wait here, please," Katie said to Syndercombe. "They must be nearby if they moored the boat here. We're going inland to search these woods on foot."

Syndercombe nodded grimly. Katie jumped off the boat, the water surging over her shoes as she jogged to land. Behind her, Leblanc followed.

They power-walked up the track that led into the woods. As Leblanc walked, he noticed two sets of footprints ahead traversing a muddy patch.

One was smaller, lighter, the prints of a woman's boots.

And the other was heavier and larger. Those prints were without a doubt the same sole tread that had been picked up at the previous crime scenes. Leblanc didn't have a measuring tape on him but they looked to be the same size, too.

"Look at that," he whispered.

Katie hissed in a breath. They both knew what it meant.

They stood still, frozen to the spot, staring at the prints heading inland.

"So he's here," Leblanc muttered. Their footsteps crunching on the forest floor, they broke into a run, knowing that they were in a race against time.

The light was dull. And the woods were thick, with the undergrowth almost impenetrable.

Every few moments, Leblanc paused to listen. Each time, he heard nothing but the sounds of nature.

The path veered right, twisting down a hill on a route that he saw led back to the beach. And then, sudden movement caught his eye. Ahead were the two of them. The tall skipper and the female tourist.

The woman was in her twenties, dark and petite.

She was racing away from the skipper, crying out, seemingly terrified as he sprinted after her.

CHAPTER TWENTY EIGHT

"Stop! Police!" Katie yelled. With her gun drawn, she sprinted along the beach after the two. Leblanc, with his longer legs, was outpacing her, running ahead. She knew they were now in a race against time to reach the woman before the killer struck.

With the gusting breeze, it occurred to Katie that the man might not have heard her. Attracting his attention would slow him down. At least he'd know he'd been seen. That could prevent her death.

"Stop or I will shoot!" she yelled.

Finally, the skipper seemed to hear the words. The dark-haired man slowed and turned, staring in horror as they raced toward him.

A few moments later, Leblanc had reached him. He grabbed his shoulder and forced him down, standing over him with gun drawn. Out of the corner of her eye, Katie saw the tourist had stumbled to a stop further on, and was turning to stare in consternation at them.

"What is this? What is it?" Fraser asked. He was down on his belly on the stones, breathing hard. His voice sounded confused and incredulous.

"We're detaining you in connection with a series of crimes committed on these islands," Katie announced breathlessly, keeping her gun trained on the man as Leblanc handcuffed him.

The tourist walked hesitantly back toward them. The young woman looked terrified.

"What—what's going on?" she stammered.

"Ma'am, you are safe now. You don't need to worry. But tell me, was there a reason why you were running along the beach like that?" Katie asked.

She glanced at Fraser, noting that despite the expression of fear on his face, he was tall and surprisingly good looking.

"He said he saw a snake." The woman pointed.

Fraser nodded. "That's right. I saw a snake. I told her we'd better run, as there was one hidden nearby, alongside the path. I hate snakes."

"Me, too," the tourist said. "He sounded in a panic. I didn't know if it was venomous, or what."

From her accent, Katie thought the petite woman might be Australian. The snake story was interesting. She'd been wondering how the killer got his victims to run. She'd thought he must have threatened them directly with physical violence. But perhaps she'd been wrong and this was the ploy he'd used.

"How did you organize this boat trip?" Katie asked her, walking behind Leblanc as he hustled the tourist along.

"I came here yesterday for a family wedding. I'm staying with my older brother, who lives near here. He went to work this morning, so I walked down to the harbor and saw this skipper was advertising a special. An hour's sail with a short island hike. It was a good price, so I took it. I can't believe I was in the boat with a criminal. He didn't seem that way when I booked the sail," she shared. "But he did get weird when we reached the island. Sort of jumpy."

All the puzzle pieces were falling into place for Katie. A good-looking skipper who didn't give any signs of his true nature. A special price on short tours that allowed him to stop off at remote islands.

The modus operandi was becoming clear.

But Fraser himself was breathlessly protesting.

"You think I committed those murders?"

"We need to prove or disprove that you had the motive and opportunity to do so," Katie said.

"I'm not a killer! I've been sailing these seas for years, making a living from taking tourists around the islands. I'm not a criminal."

"We'll be questioning you at the RCMP headquarters as soon as we can." Leblanc's voice was grim.

Fraser looked flabbergasted. "You can't do this to me. It's a mistake!"

"You will need to give us a detailed account of your time when we question you. If you have an alibi for the times of the crimes then there will be no need to take this further."

Katie didn't miss the look of blankness on Fraser's face as Leblanc said those words.

"Times of the crimes? Hang on, so I must account for all my activities in the past couple of days?"

Katie didn't expect this man to have any real alibi for the times in question. Every piece of evidence so far was pointing to his guilt, and now all that needed to be done was to gather the proof.

"Leblanc, I think you should stay behind with the tourist. The speedboat is too small for all of us, and I don't want this tourist in proximity to a suspected killer any longer. The police will need to check and search Fraser's boat for any trace evidence. And also, seize that spear and take it in for forensic examination. They can give you a ride to shore when they arrive."

"Good idea," Leblanc said. "I'll call ahead and organize for them to do the search, and I'll also ask Callum for a police car to be waiting at the harbor when you arrive, so that Fraser can be taken straight in for questioning."

Katie and Syndercombe helped the handcuffed man into the smaller speedboat. With his hands behind his back, it was difficult for him to balance as he climbed in. Katie sat him down on one of the benches and then sat next to him, keeping a firm hold on his arm.

"What times are you talking about? What alibi do you need?" Fraser blustered, as the harbormaster started up the speedboat and headed back to the harbor. "I already told you I saw a snake in the forest back there. My alarm bells went off and I knew I had to get out of there as fast as possible. I was terrified for the girl's safety. I just wanted to get her back to the boat and away from the danger."

"What times were you down at the harbor over the past few days? What times did you take tourists out on boats?" Katie asked sternly. The skipper sat silent as Katie pressed on. "Can you account for your time outside of when you were on the boat?"

"I—I don't have to tell you anything," he muttered furiously.

"Do you recall the times?" she asked again.

"I—I was down at the harbor every day," he said. "For a few hours in the mornings and then again in the afternoons and evenings. I was making the most of the tourist season, getting people out on the water and to the islands. Look, I do a lot of cash deals. I've been too busy to keep the books up to date. I'm not sure I can provide you with exact records of who I took out when."

"Did you speak to anyone down at the harbor?" Katie pressed. "Any locals or tourists?"

"You are wasting your time, you know," Fraser said. "I won't say anything. You can't make me. And you can't prove anything, can you? You can't prove any of this. I am innocent."

Fraser sounded stubborn and defiant. Katie had a feeling it was going to be a long and difficult interrogation when they reached shore.

But she knew that behind that outraged façade was a killer. And he was about to be revealed for what he was.

Once more, Katie's mind drifted back to analyzing the evidence.

"We'll have forensic evidence," she said quietly, thinking of the fishing spear.

Although, as her mind went back to that spear, Katie picked up a small inconsistency in her own thought processes. It wasn't much, but it was enough to make her uneasy.

The spear had been on the boat. The skipper hadn't been carrying it. All the evidence from the previous kills pointed to the fact that the killer had attacked his victims from behind while pursuing them.

But maybe this time, he'd decided to work a different way, Katie thought.

Even so, she could already see that this man was not going to cooperate or confess. And they could definitely not afford another mistake.

She guessed she had about an hour until Leblanc had wrapped up his side of the operations on the island and would be able to join her at the police station for the formal interrogation.

Fraser was giving vague, evasive answers. His recall of his clients was poor, and although she didn't know if this was deliberate or not, this was certainly going to be an issue.

But what if he was telling the truth? Katie suddenly wondered. He might not be blameless, he might have had issues with tourists, but what if he was genuinely not their man? The evidence was pointing to it, but she didn't want a repeat of what had played out with Sweeney.

They could not afford to arrest the wrong person again. Katie knew their careers depended on it.

Katie decided that when they reached the mainland and the police picked Fraser up, she was not going to head straight to the police department with them.

Callum could process him and take him to the interview room. In the meantime, while she waited for Leblanc, she had an hour to take a last look around, ask some more questions, and see if there were any other leads, or any other angles, that they might have missed.

CHAPTER TWENTY NINE

As the police car drove off, heading for the RCMP offices, Katie watched it go, feeling frustrated. She wanted to be sure of this suspect. One hundred percent sure. And she wasn't. She wished she could set her doubts aside and go straight to the police department with confidence.

But her mind kept confronting her with the weak points in the case against Fraser.

Was it really so incriminating that a skipper who took tourists out on the water would have a fishing spear in his boat? And why had it been in his boat and not on his person, if he'd intended to murder the dark-haired tourist as she'd run?

Perhaps his neighbor in the docks, Heath, might be able to fill in some of the gaps in his account of the past couple of days, Katie decided, striding down the walkway.

Heath was busy mooring the small speedboat in place. Katie guessed that Syndercombe had taken it straight back to his berth, after dropping them at the main pier where the police had been waiting to pick up Fraser.

"Heath," she called.

"Yes, sure? What is it?" he asked inquiringly. "Do you need my boat again?"

"No. I was hoping to get some more background on Fraser. Can you tell me about his comings and goings over the past few days?"

Heath made a face. "Unfortunately not. I've been on a two-day cruise with a group of guests, overnighting at different hotels along the coast. So I haven't been here at all. We got back early this morning."

Katie tried another angle.

"There was an incident a while ago where he apparently abandoned a tourist on an island. Do you know anything about that?"

"Oh, yes. Yes, I do. Fraser took the fall for that, all right," Heath said thoughtfully.

"What happened?" Katie said, raising internal eyebrows at the news there were clearly two sides to this story.

"He told me about it afterward. It was a difficult situation. There was a husband and wife on the boat, and the husband was out of control. He was drunk and abusive and threatening her. Fraser said he decided to leave the husband on the island to cool off. It wasn't a decision he wanted to make, but he was worried about the safety of the wife, and also the three other passengers aboard who were very upset by this and didn't feel comfortable with him on board."

"And then what happened?"

"He dropped the wife and other clients on shore. Then he went straight back for the husband. But of course, the man decided to be vindictive. He laid a complaint and twisted the facts. The wife went along with it and confirmed the husband's story. She was an abused wife for sure, and must have been forced to. And Fraser keeps poor records, he's careless that way. So he couldn't contact the other guests to confirm his side of the story, as he had no idea who they were."

"I see," Katie said.

"It was a really unfortunate set of circumstances. I felt bad for him. He was only trying to do the right thing, protect a woman and look after the other guests, but he ended up having to pay a substantial fine and was nearly arrested. But he moved on from it, and he told me afterward he was still glad he'd done what he did. He was really more upset about the wife than he was about himself. He used to speak about her for a while after that, and would mention to me that he hoped she was okay."

"You think he's a good guy?" Katie asked.

"He's not a bad guy. Flaky and disorganized. That's his weak point for sure. He's made some bad decisions, he carries some baggage, but hey, who doesn't? He has a good heart and he will always try and protect someone in trouble," Heath said. "He's not a people person. That can sometimes count against him, he comes across as aggressive, he doesn't handle conflict in a diplomatic way. But he tries to stand up for people, all the same."

"Does he have any particular issues? Any phobias?" Katie asked, remembering what had played out on the beach.

"Snakes," Heath said with a rueful smile. "He's got an illogical fear of them. Something to do with his past, even though I've told him before now there are only about five types of snakes in Nova Scotia and none of them are venomous. But he really gets fearful when he goes into the islands. He gets very jumpy. Always has. And of course, all the snakes come out when he's there. Honestly, I don't think I've ever seen one on a hike. He sees them all the time."

"Thanks," Katie said.

She turned away feeling even more uncertain about the supposedly strong suspect they had pinned down, now that there was an actual confirmed reason why he had told the tourist to run.

They were close. That was a certainty. They knew the killer was operating from the harbor. They knew he was taking tourists out on a boat. But were they close enough? Was it Fraser?

Katie paced along the walkway, thoughts churning in her mind as she breathed in the salty air. She tried to stay objective and guide herself along a logical path. The evidence was all there. It just needed one last piece of the jigsaw puzzle to slot into place.

Maybe it was time to take a step back and look at the bigger picture. Who was this killer?

The killer was someone who clearly had the ability to get along with others. To appeal to them. To make them a spur of the moment offer that they could not refuse, to go out on the water.

But perhaps he was not an official tour guide, but rather someone who was posing as one. If he was that type of personality, he would be able to lie easily and well. People would believe and trust him. In fact, if they'd listened to Campbell, they might have realized that sooner. The environmentalist had mentioned how many boats were taking tourists out, and that both licensed and informal tour guides were operating in the waters.

Katie felt like this was a breakthrough in her thinking.

The harbormaster had focused only on the tour guides, not on locals who owned boats. It would be easy enough for a local to get in conversation with passersby and claim to be a tour guide. Who would know the difference, as a newcomer to Nova Scotia? An unlicensed boat owner could fly under the radar, unnoticed by the harbormaster.

Making a further logical leap, she realized that for an ordinary boat owner, it would also be easy to pick up a victim after hours in a bar or restaurant. That would explain how he'd gotten Heidi to the islands late at night. A friendly chat in a bar, an offer to go out for a nighttime sail, perhaps a flirtatious invite. That would have sealed the deal, she guessed. And there were a few upmarket, tourist-friendly bars within a block or two of the harbor. Their doors were open and she saw lunch time clientele were starting to trickle in.

But on such a beautiful day, would this man be in a bar that was not yet busy?

Katie thought that the harbor was probably going to provide a better hunting ground for him on this fine, sunny day.

The tour boats were moored in an area adjacent to the privately owned boats. There was no differentiation between the two areas. There was nothing to stop tourists wandering the whole way around the harbor area.

What if she was to pose as a tourist? Katie suddenly wondered. If she strolled innocently down the area of the harbor where the other boats were moored, would he notice her and take the bait? And what would she need to do in order to ensure that the bait was authentic enough?

Katie headed over to a nearby kiosk. There, she bought a Nova Scotia T-shirt and a pink hat and scarf. She quickly retreated to the unmarked car, climbed inside, and changed.

Her gun. What to do? It was too obvious on her hip. It made her look like law enforcement and not like a tourist.

Katie took off her gun belt and locked it away in the equipment lockbox in the car's trunk. It wasn't the ideal long-term solution, but she wasn't sure if her theory would even pan out. All she wanted to do was spend an hour testing it, until it was time to meet up with Leblanc.

Now looking like a tourist, and she hoped not in the least like an FBI agent, Katie strolled along, checking out the boats as she walked.

She took out her phone and snapped a few photos, forcing herself to appear relaxed, despite the gnawing anxiety she felt inside and the lead-heavy pressure of the case. Now she needed to play a role.

If she was going to encourage this killer to take the bait, she needed to become who he expected her to be.

She smiled as she strolled, as if she was enjoying the day without a care in the world.

And then, from one of the boats she was passing, she heard a friendly, "Morning!"

Katie glanced around, reminding herself to appear casual. Her first thought was that this tall, dark-haired, good-looking man was a genuine skipper, just greeting her in passing. He looked preoccupied with his task of polishing the boat's gleaming rail.

It was a handsome boat that looked in excellent condition. Its name was written in black lettering on its side. *The Osprey*.

"Morning," she replied. She then reminded herself that she should not take anyone for granted, and that she should check him out more carefully.

As she was figuring out a way to continue with the conversation, he spoke again.

"Are you by any chance staying at the Ocean Lodge?" His blue eyes met hers, cheerful and sparkling.

"No. I'm not staying there. Why?" she asked.

He sighed. "I had a booking come in yesterday from a woman who said she'd be checking in there this morning. She wanted to go for an hour's cruise. She hasn't arrived yet. She said she'd be here at eleven, and it's already after midday. I wondered if you were possibly her."

Now, Katie felt more intrigued. This was checking all the boxes. Finding out if she was a tourist. Broaching the subject of the hour's cruise even though this was not in the tour boat area.

Deciding to keep exploring this last-ditch possibility, she smiled back at him.

"I'm not her. My name's Katie Winter. Who are you?"

"I'm Garrison," he replied with a grin. "And I'm very pleased to meet you."

CHAPTER THIRTY

"Garrison?" Katie repeated, looking at him closely. He smiled mildly. She saw only friendly innocence in his eyes.

"Half name, half nickname," the tall man replied with a deprecating shrug.

"And you hire out boats?" Katie then asked, wondering if he was going to take this further.

"I do, yes."

"Are you a tour operator?" She wanted to see what he'd say to that.

"No. I'm a just a regular boat owner. I had a tour guide's license a couple of years ago, and worked part time. I did quite a lot of advertising and marketing. I still get calls, and referrals from old clients. But I'm not in the game officially any longer."

"How did this woman know about you?"

"She was referred to me by a previous client. I agreed to take her out. But she clearly had other plans. I'm not worried. It was a great excuse to come down here and tidy up the boat a bit."

"You came down here specially?" Katie asked.

"Yes. I booked the morning off work—I'm a mobile handyman so I work for myself, but I like to be available in business hours for call-outs. If she had turned up, I would have taken her out and then gone back to work. But at the moment, I don't mind the wasted time. I feel it's important to spend time down here."

"Why?" Katie asked.

"You know, I want to look after people. I've heard about this killer out there. You may have heard, too. I've seen warnings in some of the hotels." He sounded seriously worried.

"You have?" Katie was stunned he'd mentioned it. Would he have mentioned this so blatantly if he was the killer? It cast doubt in her mind all over again.

"Yes. It's part of the reason I've been honoring all the bookings I can. I'm worried. I love this place. I love our tourism industry. I can't bear to see it destroyed. Every time I go out on the boat, I look all around the islands. Look for boats. See who's moored there. I feel somehow, maybe I can try and prevent it happening again. And of course, if someone goes out with me, at least I know they're safe. I'm a good sailor. Careful. And I look after my clients."

Now Katie wondered if he might be selling himself just a little too hard. Or was it just genuine concern driving him?

If this man was the killer he was highly intelligent, extroverted, and with a level of empathy she'd not expected. It was extremely unusual.

Katie knew she had only a moment to decide and she had to play the part she was now committed to.

There was only one way she could find out more. It was time to see what would happen if she asked for a boat ride.

"I don't have much time. Only an hour. But I'd love to go out on the water, so if you're planning on a sail, can I take the booking?"

Being on the boat might help her learn more. If he was the killer she couldn't afford to walk away. If he wasn't, she'd only spend sixty minutes ruling him out. She could check out the boat. See if there was a weapon on board. And she'd message Leblanc immediately and tell him where she was. That way he could follow them and ensure she didn't come to any harm.

She had a feeling about this man. He was manipulating her into this. Subtly, skillfully, but he was doing it at a level where he was making it seem like her idea. There were all skills the killer would need in order to do what he had done.

"Of course. I was planning to go out for an hour or so anyway. You're welcome to join me. It would be my pleasure to have you along."

"I can't accept a free ride," Katie said. "Whatever you were going to charge your client, I will pay. Surely that's fair? I don't believe in taking something for free, if it costs money."

He stared at her, frowning. Katie had the sense there was a lot going on in his mind. She wished she could read his thoughts.

"I was going to ask you about that," he said. "That was the question I was going to ask. But you beat me to it."

"That's strange," Katie said, laughing.

"I don't really feel I need to accept money from you, but on the other hand, I have lost a fee that was important to me. Shall we say a third of the original rate? That would be twenty dollars?"

Katie looked in her wallet and handed the money over. She felt lightheaded with tension and anticipation.

They climbed into the boat and Garrison started up the motor and headed out to sea. She stood on the deck, looking around, taking in the boat.

Her eyes were drawn to a steel fishing spear on a bracket on the side. It was three-pronged, she noted, narrowing her eyes. But it was stacked on a bracket behind other fishing equipment. A smaller spear, a net, a few rods, a bait and tackle box. There was a reason for its presence. It looked clean and new. It looked as if it hadn't been touched for a while, stashed away at the back of everything on that holder.

But Katie knew only too well that appearances could deceive.

"Do you fish?" she asked.

"No. It's not my hobby. But I have clients who fish. When I took tourists out full time, they wanted a well-equipped boat, although most tourists do think they can fish better than they actually can."

"And what about the spear?" Katie wanted to make the most of her opportunity. She wanted to watch Garrison's reaction to the question, to see if it told her anything at all.

He laughed. "That's very seldom used. A client asked me to keep it. He'd bought a new spear and he didn't want it or need it anymore."

"So you brought it back?"

"Yes. The spear's basically just for show. It's a conversation piece. Very few tourists do big game fishing that requires it. The client who gave it to me was actually a local."

Katie nodded, her mind racing. The answers were plausible. Garrison seemed untroubled. What he was saying confirmed what the fishing store owner had said. And yet there had been a moment, just one moment when she'd mentioned the spear, when she'd seen his face change.

She might have been imagining it.

But just for an instant he'd seemed to be a different person. Even though it was subtle, she was sure she'd seen it.

She glanced at Garrison, standing at the wheel, now looking out to sea. His back was to her. Trusting.

Katie paced away, deciding she was going to use the moment to message Leblanc. He needed to know where she was and what she was doing. Despite his air of innocence, it would be worth bringing Garrison in for questioning and asking him about his movements over the past few days.

If it ruled him out, well and good.

If it didn't—Katie thought again of that moment when she thought she'd seen something different in his eyes. If it didn't rule him out, at least she would have backup to make the arrest.

She thought again of that glimpse.

That fishing spear was tucked away in brackets, behind other equipment. He couldn't get to it easily. But there was nothing stopping him having another stashed away in a different place.

She knew she could defend herself physically from most attackers. She was experienced and trained. But there was no reason to put herself at undue risk.

She turned away from him and quickly keyed in the message.

"I'm on a boat with a possible suspect. Name of Garrison. We left Halifax harbor 5 mins ago, sailing south east. Boat's name is The Osprey. It's about thirty feet, white and blue."

Katie read the message once more before sending it. It was time to turn back to Garrison and continue playing the part of tourist. But as her finger hit the Send button, a fist slammed into her head.

The blow was powerful, painful, and utterly shocking. The phone flew out of her hand. It tumbled across the deck and splashed into the sea below.

She felt dizzy. She couldn't balance. The world was blurring.

Then the fist slammed into her again, and everything went dark.

CHAPTER THIRTY ONE

Light filtered back into Katie's world, together with a blinding headache. She didn't think she'd been out for long. She had groggy memories of being dragged off the boat, of stones scratching her legs.

Now, the sun was shining above her and the waves were crashing somewhere near.

She opened her eyes, blinking painfully.

She was lying on her side behind a large rocky outcrop near a beach. She could feel the coarse pebbles beneath her body. Looking down, she saw that her hands were tied behind her back. The rope was tight. It was cutting into her skin.

She felt utterly confused. How had this happened? He'd seemed trusting of her. He'd had his back to her! How had he even noticed her sending a quick text, and why on earth had he attacked?

A shadow fell over her

Looking up, Katie saw Garrison standing in front of her.

He looked furious, but as Katie blinked at him, she thought it was more than that. Something had changed in his face. He was not the man she'd been talking to on the boat. He was the one she'd glimpsed.

Now, his eyes burned with a cold fire.

She'd made a mistake that was going to cost her. For just one moment she'd taken her attention away from him, not knowing that he suspected her just as strongly as she'd suspected him.

"I didn't trust you. I didn't trust you from the start. I thought you were plainclothes. But you were too good. Too convincing. You fooled me, until I saw you bent over your phone like that. I read your body language. And when you were out cold, I found your badge. I knew I was right."

Katie couldn't risk saying anything. She stared at him in silence.

"You wanted to make me think you were someone else. But you've been a cop all along." He leaned toward her. "So what I need to know now is who were you messaging? What did you say? Your phone went into the water before I could check it. I'm normally fast on that kind of thing."

She shrugged. "I said a couple of things. If you wanted to know, the best decision would have been not to hit me so hard you made me drop it."

He grimaced. She could see rage in his eyes and fear, too.

"Nobody gets the better of me that way. Nobody gets the jump on me. Not without paying for it, big-time. Who were you messaging? What did you say?"

Katie thought quickly.

Garrison was calm on the outside. But he was badly shaken. He was desperate to get information. The problem was that she knew this was going to end one way.

With her death.

That was the only way it could end, and she wasn't even sure the text to Leblanc would have had time to send. But there were still choices. Her death could be slow or it could be quick. Garrison seemed to like a build-up before he unleashed his violence.

So Katie needed to buy time now. She needed to figure out how she could manipulate him to keep her alive as long as possible.

Even if Leblanc didn't come to help her in time, a swimmer or a boater might see something. A cry for help might reach someone's ears.

Her eyes moved over to the knife in his belt.

The fishing spear was nowhere to be seen. Not yet. She thought that he would need it. It represented the other half of who he was. The half he was becoming now.

"I'm going to ask you again. Who were you messaging? And what did you say?" He took a step toward her.

"Why should I tell you?" Katie asked.

"Because you're going to pay for what you've done. You're going to pay for being a cop. You're going to pay for all of this."

Katie said nothing.

It was hard to see a way out. She could sense that she was in trouble. At any moment he could unleash the brutal violence that he'd already shown. But she was trying to stay calm.

"I just need to know. Who did you call? What did you say? That's the question. That's the new question."

His eyes narrowed as he stared at her.

Katie felt this question was somehow important to him. It had weight. It would influence his decisions. It was part of his ritual. He'd decide on a different course of action depending on what she said.

She had no doubt that in his twisted mind the right answer would spare her. But she had the feeling it was likely to be difficult to give that answer.

"Why does it matter so much to you?" she said, deciding to play him at his own game. "You clearly have a scenario planned out in your mind, depending on what I say. One response means you will do one thing. Another response means something different. Probably, there's one very unlikely answer that means you will spare me."

She saw the uncertainty in his eyes, but also the anger that she'd read him.

"I think you're working to a kind of checklist," Katie said. "Something you've constructed in your head. I don't know what will happen if I give you the wrong answer. I don't think it will be good for me. But I'm willing to take the risk."

He stared at her. His face was hard, but his eyes were moving fast. She was unbalancing him. She was messing with the step-by-step sequence of events he was planning on. But she had no idea whether that was a good or bad thing.

"You need to answer me, Katie Winter. Just give me the answer."

"The answer is that I don't know," she told him. "I have no idea if the message went through. You saw that. You're a clever guy. You saw what happened as I tried to send it."

"Let's assume it was sent. Who was it sent to?"

"Someone close to me."

"Did you tell them where I was?"

Katie's mind raced. This was like a game of chess and if she thought far enough ahead, she could get the outcome she wanted.

Getting into a killer's mind had never been more important.

Finally, she made her decision.

"I messaged my case partner. He's close to me. And yes, I told him where I was. I told him to drop everything and come to help me. He expects that he will be helping to arrest you."

As she spoke, she tugged at the ties. If only they would loosen. But he'd fastened them with all the strength that a good skipper would put into his work.

He stared down at her, smiling slightly.

"A good answer," he said. "But not the one that will spare you."

He turned and walked away, striding back along the beach in the direction of the boat.

She knew where he was going now.

He was going to get the fishing spear, but he wasn't going to kill her. Not yet. He was going to wait for Leblanc. He was going to ambush him.

He wanted to kill both of them. Then, no doubt, he would make a run for it and disappear. But he didn't know how good Leblanc was. Or how closely he understood Katie.

Together, Katie hoped, they could take him down and save themselves.

CHAPTER THIRTY TWO

Standing in the motorboat belonging to Heath, which he'd just borrowed again, Leblanc forged across the sea. He felt desperate. His hands were tight on the controls. He hoped he was heading in Katie's direction but given the fact her phone was now off, the killer might have overpowered her.

Anxiety flared inside him. He had no idea if she was still alive. He'd checked two islands so far, and there had been no sign of her. Time was running out.

He'd gotten the text just as he'd reached Halifax. He'd sprinted straight for the boat. Out on the sea, he'd called Callum, who was now organizing a massive raid, with police backup.

Leblanc had decided to start the search immediately, without waiting for the police.

He thought he knew what to look out for. He knew the name of the boat. He knew the approximate location.

And he knew the killer's habits. He would moor the boat somewhere out of the way and then, Leblanc was sure, he would take Katie onto shore.

But so far, there had been no sign of her, and he was worried that he was going too far, or had taken the wrong route. He felt a sense of doom. This killer might have attacked her. Hurt her. That was why her phone wasn't on.

But Katie was smart. She would have fought back. Physically, but also mentally. She would have done her utmost to stay alive.

Leblanc eased off on the throttle.

This island was his last hope. It was further to the west than he thought she could have gone, but perhaps the killer had veered away with her, hoping to go unnoticed.

With his heart thumping, he stood as tall as he could in the boat to see over the bobbing waves.

And he saw her. He saw her!

A small figure, prone on the pebbles, wriggling her foot from behind the rocks where he must have dumped her. Doing her best to be seen by anyone passing by.

Relief, amazement, euphoria filled him. She was alive! She was tied up and as he sailed closer, he also saw she'd been gagged. He needed to get to her now, before the killer returned.

Leblanc maneuvered the boat alongside the rocks and jumped out, wading through thigh-high, icy water.

"Katie," he called. "Katie!"

He reached the beach, feeling gritty rock under his shoes. He rushed up to her. But, as he neared her, he saw the warning in her eyes. A narrowed glance.

A flick of her head to the side.

A moment later, he was aware of movement from that direction, and he realized what she'd been warning him about.

Someone was waiting, hidden behind the rock.

He had only a moment to jackknife sideways, but it was enough to save his life.

A big, bearded man leaped out, wielding a heavy, steel fishing spear. But thanks to Leblanc's evasive action, the spear didn't strike into his core.

Instead, the barbed shaft nicked his side, winging him just under his ribcage, but not penetrating beyond the skin.

He felt the impact immediately. Shallow as it was, the blow was hard and sharp. The pain was a white-hot flame.

He doubled over in agony, glancing at his attacker. This maniac, this murderer, was Garrison. Desperately, he grabbed the shaft of the heavy weapon. He couldn't risk Garrison using it again. He tugged it away from him, pulling as hard as he could.

Garrison's face was twisted. His eyes were dead and empty.

Abandoning the spear, he attacked Leblanc, flinging himself onto him, and Leblanc knew he would have to fight for his life to survive.

Garrison was strong, but also insane. Leblanc knew that injured as he was, he was in serious trouble. Garrison threw himself down, using his weight to pin Leblanc to the ground. His big, strong hands were clawing at Leblanc's face. He was going for the weak points, trying to damage his eyes. Leblanc twisted away from him, bringing his knee up, hoping to cause pain and damage.

Garrison was snarling threats. "I'm going to kill you, you bastard! I'm going to kill you."

Leblanc needed to get this maniac off him. He was in pain, and the wound was bleeding more heavily than he'd expected it to. It was gushing blood.

Summoning all his strength, he met his attacker full in the face, managing to whack him on the nose with a head butt. Garrison yelled out, more in surprise than in pain, but for a moment, he was stunned.

Leblanc reached up and pushed as hard as he could against Garrison's neck, digging his fingers in, trying to achieve an effective stranglehold. Garrison grabbed his wrists with one hand and tried to throw him off. But Leblanc hung on. He held on to Garrison's arms and pushed down hard with all his weight, trying to keep his grip as the other man's strength bore down on him.

Leblanc wasn't going to be able to hold him for long. He was hurting too much. He was starting to weaken. Now the fight was going against him. Garrison wrenched Leblanc's hands off his neck and hissed in triumph.

But then he saw what Katie was doing. Out of the corner of his eye, he caught a glimpse of her.

She had managed to crawl over to the discarded fishing spear, and she was using its wicked, barbed edge to cut through her ropes, slowly and patiently.

Leblanc shouted loudly, keeping Garrison's attention on him. With the last of his strength he writhed away, trying to lead Garrison in a direction where his back would be toward Katie.

He took a punch to the jaw that made him see stars. His head lashed back onto the pebbles.

Laughing manically, Garrison raised his fist again. This time, Leblanc knew, it would hit him directly in the face. This was going to hurt. It was probably going to kill. He'd fought all the way to the wire, but now it was over.

And then, from behind him, he heard a dull, thudding noise.

As if in a dream, he watched the rock smash into Garrison's head. Katie had gotten herself free. She'd managed to get out of her ropes. And just in time, she'd managed to save him.

Garrison's eyes lost their light and focus. He sprawled forward as Leblanc writhed out of the way.

He got to his hands and knees, gasping. He was streaked with mud and blood. But they were alive. And Garrison was down.

Fumbling with the handcuffs on his belt, he got them around the man's thick wrists.

Katie ripped the gag out of her mouth. She ran over to Leblanc.

"Are you okay?" she asked, concern thrumming in her voice. "You're bleeding."

"I'm okay," he gasped.

"We need to get you to the hospital," she said.

He tried to smile, pressing a hand on the wound in his side. It hurt like hell, but at least now he had a chance to control the bleeding.

"Help is coming," he said.

He looked out to sea, and at that moment, he saw the boats on the horizon. Police and Coast Guard were on their way.

Together, they had done it. They had managed to capture one of the most evilly intelligent killers they had ever been pitted against.

Their partnership was what had saved them.

Slowly, painfully, he limped to the shore and lifted his arm, ready to alert the forces that would take them back to safety.

CHAPTER THIRTY THREE

Katie sat in the boat next to the handcuffed Garrison, feeling bruised and battered, but deeply relieved that they had finally arrested the correct suspect. The one they needed. The one whose life imprisonment would finally close this heartbreaking case.

Nothing more than instinct, and an illogical determination to pursue all possible leads, had prompted her to keep looking further, even with a tour captain in custody and a set of circumstances that almost, but not quite, fit the crime.

If she had settled for Fraser she would never have taken that last walk down the dock and met up with Garrison. This evil, violent predator would still be out there.

Spray stung her face as the boat powered toward land.

Glancing at Garrison, Katie saw with a shock that he had regained consciousness and was watching her. There was an unexpected expression in his blue eyes.

Was it amusement?

It chilled her. It was not the expression she'd expected to see there.

"Well done, Katie," he said in a low voice that only she could hear. "You did a sterling job."

She stared at him, wondering if she should engage in conversation. It almost seemed as if he had something to share.

"It's a pity you and I couldn't have met under different circumstances," he said. "Because, in a strange way, I like you. Even though you've temporarily inconvenienced me. You know, I wouldn't have killed you if you hadn't messaged your partner. You answered the first question right. Not many people do that."

Katie's eyes widened.

"Temporarily inconvenienced?" You're going to be in prison for life. No hope of parole. You'll never get out."

"I have learned in life there is no such thing as never," Garrison said quietly. "So if you really want to know, I plan to get out. I'm going to do it. I will make it possible."

"Don't even think about it," Katie said. "I'll never let it happen. We're going to keep you behind bars forever."

Garrison laughed at that, and she saw he was genuinely amused.

"I look forward to the challenge," he said. "Don't worry, Agent. I'll be a model prisoner. I'll make friends with all the guards and other inmates. I'll live quietly in my cell. Until, one day—I won't be there anymore."

Katie shivered. She couldn't help herself.

"I've been doing this a long, long time. Longer than you know," he continued. "Off the record, I could point islands out to you where you would find proof of that. A surprising amount of proof. Of course, only I know where they are. Just bones by now. Just bones. But lots of them. Look long enough and you'll find them. You see, it's so easy to make tourists disappear. People on their own. Lost, and never found."

"Will you tell me?" Katie asked. This conversation felt creepy and intimate.

Garrison considered.

"No," he said. "I won't even admit to it again."

"Why did you start leaving the bodies in full view?"

He shrugged. "It was more fun. Better shock value, you know? I guess I got a little ahead of myself. I thought you'd never catch me. I'm still surprised you did, eventually. That's why I thought I'd give you a heads-up. Just between you and me. The bodies are out there. More of them than you think. It's been my little secret, but now I'm telling you, too. You see, Katie—I like you."

He turned away and stared at the horizon.

He looked more as if he was on a cruise, than on a Coast Guard speedboat heading for a maximum security cell.

Again, Katie felt a chill. But she was going to listen to what he said. She was going to take it seriously, because she didn't think this killer was lying. Day by day, island by island, she knew that Callum and his team would diligently search, looking to uncover the evidence of earlier murders.

But for now, it was time to join up with Leblanc, who'd remained on the island to get his wound treated. Her heart lifted as she saw the medic's helicopter cutting through the sky, coming in to land.

*

Late that evening, Katie and Leblanc boarded the plane that would take them back home to Sault Ste. Marie. Leblanc was still walking awkwardly and she was sure his injury would take a week or two to fully heal.

But Katie thought, in his eyes, she saw a level of calmness and decisiveness that had not been there for a long while. This case had been wrapped up, rock solid. They had their suspect locked up in prison. They'd learned his real name, Hamish Waters, and his background. He'd been a soldier, but had been dishonorably discharged from the service. He'd taken a few odd jobs around town. He had inherited family money from his mother, who had mysteriously drowned a few years ago in what appeared to be a sailing accident.

Katie wondered if she'd been his very first kill. She was sure other bodies would be found soon. Callum and his team were organizing a methodical search of all the islands over the next few weeks.

They sat down and put on their seatbelts.

"When I was packing up to leave just now, I took a moment to email Paris," he said in a low voice.

"Oh?" Katie felt a flare of anxiety for the implications of this.

"I told them that I was hugely grateful for the job offer. But that after serious thought, I was going to remain with the task force."

Katie felt relief overwhelm her. Suddenly, the world seemed a brighter place.

"I'm sorry about the way I behaved," he continued. "I crossed a line. I should never have done what I did. I was running out of choices. I was committed to something that I now see would have destroyed me. I can't thank you enough for showing me what I was becoming. It won't happen again, Katie. I promise."

Katie took a deep breath.

"We all make mistakes," she said. "It's in the past now."

"I can't imagine having any other partner. I never want to work with anyone else. I hope that you'll forgive me."

"I already have," Katie said.

Finally, she felt at peace, and that Leblanc had made the right decision. For himself, and also for her.

And there was nothing to forgive, not really. Katie knew only too well, from personal experience, what it took to conquer the demons of the past.

EPILOGUE

Katie jerked awake, breathing hard, erupting with a cry from the clutches of one of the most intense nightmares she'd had in a while.

She sat up in bed, her hands shaking, reaching for the light to banish the shadows. Breathing deeply, she reminded herself she was at home in Sault Ste. Marie, in her own bed.

But for a moment, she hadn't been.

She'd been on the riverbank, listening to its frothy roar, watching the sky overhead, dark with clouds.

And she'd seen a man approaching.

A tall, bearded man. Exactly like the person Everton had described.

Except this time, Katie recognized him.

Deep in her mind, her subconscious had been at work. Finally, she had realized who this person was. She had known him, long ago.

Goose bumps prickled her arms. Everton could surely not have been making this up? Not if Katie had now linked the description to a real person.

A name flitted into her mind, almost forgotten, on the edges of memory.

Gabriel Rath. That was who he was.

Gabriel Rath. A homesteader who'd lived outside town, who'd occasionally come by her father's place to rent a fishing boat. For some reason, he'd always made Katie feel a little afraid. A little uneasy. That was what she recalled most about him. Not his looks, but her own instinctive reaction to him.

The weird thing was that she didn't recall seeing him at all after her sister's disappearance.

Katie got out of bed. It was still dark. Not even five a.m. But there was no more time to waste.

She was going to take the next step on the hunt for the truth. She was going to track down Gabriel Rath and find out where he was now.

NOW AVAILABLE!

<u>HOLD ME</u>
(A Katie Winter FBI Suspense Thriller—Book 7)

When a hitchhiker narrowly escapes from a murderous, lone trucker in the vast Canadian wilderness, FBI Special Agent Katie Winter realizes there isn't much time to catch this new serial killer before he strikes again.

"Molly Black has written a taut thriller that will keep you on the edge of your seat… I absolutely loved this book and can't wait to read the next book in the series!"
—Reader review for Girl One: Murder

HOLD ME is book #7 in a new series by #1 bestselling mystery and suspense author Molly Black.

FBI Special Agent Katie Winter is no stranger to frigid winters, isolation, and dangerous cases. With her sterling record of hunting down serial killers, she is a fast-rising star in the BAU, and Katie is the natural choice to partner with Canadian law enforcement to track killers across brutal and unforgiving landscapes.

A page-turning and harrowing crime thriller featuring a brilliant and tortured FBI agent, the KATIE WINTER series is a riveting mystery, packed with non-stop action, suspense, twists and turns, revelations, and driven by a breakneck pace that will keep you flipping pages late into the night. Fans of Rachel Caine, Teresa Driscoll and Robert Dugoni are sure to fall in love.

Books #8 and #9 in the series—PROTECT ME and REMEMBER ME—are now also available!

"I binge read this book. It hooked me in and didn't stop till the last few pages… I look forward to reading more!"

—Reader review for Found You

“I loved this book! Fast-paced plot, great characters and interesting insights into investigating cold cases. I can't wait to read the next book!”
—Reader review for Girl One: Murder

“Very good book… You will feel like you are right there looking for the kidnapper! I know I will be reading more in this series!”
—Reader review for Girl One: Murder

“This is a very well written book and holds your interest from page 1… Definitely looking forward to reading the next one in the series, and hopefully others as well!”
—Reader review for Girl One: Murder

“Wow, I cannot wait for the next in this series. Starts with a bang and just keeps going.”
—Reader review for Girl One: Murder

“Well written book with a great plot, one that will keep you up at night. A page turner!”
—Reader review for Girl One: Murder

“A great suspense that keeps you reading… can't wait for the next in this series!”
—Reader review for Found You

“Sooo soo good! There are a few unforeseen twists… I binge read this like I binge watch Netflix. It just sucks you in.”
—Reader review for Found You

Molly Black

Bestselling author Molly Black is author of the MAYA GRAY FBI suspense thriller series, comprising nine books (and counting); of the RYLIE WOLF FBI suspense thriller series, comprising six books (and counting); of the TAYLOR SAGE FBI suspense thriller series, comprising six books (and counting); and of the KATIE WINTER FBI suspense thriller series, comprising nine books (and counting).

An avid reader and lifelong fan of the mystery and thriller genres, Molly loves to hear from you, so please feel free to visit www.mollyblackauthor.com to learn more and stay in touch.

BOOKS BY MOLLY BLACK

MAYA GRAY MYSTERY SERIES
GIRL ONE: MURDER (Book #1)
GIRL TWO: TAKEN (Book #2)
GIRL THREE: TRAPPED (Book #3)
GIRL FOUR: LURED (Book #4)
GIRL FIVE: BOUND (Book #5)
GIRL SIX: FORSAKEN (Book #6)
GIRL SEVEN: CRAVED (Book #7)
GIRL EIGHT: HUNTED (Book #8)
GIRL NINE: GONE (Book #9)

RYLIE WOLF FBI SUSPENSE THRILLER
FOUND YOU (Book #1)
CAUGHT YOU (Book #2)
SEE YOU (Book #3)
WANT YOU (Book #4)
TAKE YOU (Book #5)
DARE YOU (Book #6)

TAYLOR SAGE FBI SUSPENSE THRILLER
DON'T LOOK (Book #1)
DON'T BREATHE (Book #2)
DON'T RUN (Book #3)
DON'T FLINCH (Book #4)
DON'T REMEMBER (Book #5)
DON'T TELL (Book #6)

KATIE WINTER FBI SUSPENSE THRILLER
SAVE ME (Book #1)
REACH ME (Book #2)
HIDE ME (Book #3)
BELIEVE ME (Book #4)
HELP ME (Book #5)
FORGET ME (Book #6)
HOLD ME (Book #7)

PROTECT ME (Book #8)
REMEMBER ME (Book #9)

www.ingramcontent.com/pod-product-compliance
Lightning Source LLC
Chambersburg PA
CBHW030614310726
48979CB00003B/707

9781094395036